"He is justly rated as one of the nation's m~~~' writers."
Tim~

Wilfrid Sheed wa~ 1930. His
parents were the v~ ~ and Maisie
Ward Sheed, foun~ ~m Sheed and Ward.

He was educated ~~ Academy and Oxford. In the
late 1950s he began writing about movies for *Jubilee* in New
York, and later was the drama critic and book editor for *Commonweal*. His reviews and essays have appeared in many magazines and newspapers, including *The Atlantic, Esquire, GQ, Life, The New York Times Book Review*, and *Sports Illustrated*.

His novels *Office Politics* (1966), *Max Jamison* (1970) and *People Will Always Be Kind* (1973) were nominated for National Book Awards; he has also been nominated for the National Book Critics' Circle Award in criticism.

His other novels are: *A Middle Class Education* (1960); *The Hack* (1963); *Square's Progress* (1965); *The Blacking Factory & Pennsylvania Gothic: A Short Novel and a Long Story* (1968); *Transatlantic Blues* (1978); and *The Boys of Winter* (1987).

His essays, articles, and reviews have been collected in several volumes: *The Morning After* (1971), *The Good Word & Other Words* (1978); *Essays in Disguise* (1990). Among his other works of nonfiction are *Muhammad Ali: A Portrait in Words and Photographs* (1975); *Clare Booth Luce* (1982); *Frank & Maisie: A Memoir with Parents* (1985); *Baseball and Lesser Sports* (1991); and *My Life as a Fan* (1993). His "memoir of recovery," *In Love with Daylight* (1995), is available in A COMMON READER EDITION.

He has received a Guggenheim fellowship, an award in literature from the National Institute and American Academy, and a Grammy Award for his liner notes to *The Voice: Frank Sinatra, The Columbia Years 1943–52*. From 1972 until 1988 he was a member of the Book-of-the-Month Club editorial board.

Wilfrid Sheed and his wife, the writer Miriam Ungerer, live in Sag Harbor, New York.

Max
Jamison

a novel by
Wilfrid Sheed

A COMMON READER EDITION
THE AKADINE PRESS
2001

Max Jamison

A COMMON READER EDITION published 2001 by The
Akadine Press Inc., by arrangement with the author.

A Common Reader Edition and fountain colophon
are trademarks of The Akadine Press, Inc.

ISBN 1-58579-039-7

10 9 8 7 6 5 4 3 2 1

part one

1

It's all very fine to say smoking in the lobby only, but have you seen the lobby lately? The woman in the black dress just stood staring at his black shiny shoes. There was no reasoning with her. He pushed along behind the crowd, trying not to burn anyone's dinner jacket, and through the doors, where the audience congealed on him suddenly and almost flung him back into the no-smoking zone.

Beyond the lobby there lurked a cold night and a sharp black wind. Maybe even some snow on it; inside, jammed in a hazy defile, were at least five people he didn't want to see—starting, he now knew for sure, with the author, Sam Melman, and his wife Rose. What one went through for a cigarette.

"What do you think?" whispered Jack Flashman. "Lousy, huh?"

He looked around severely. He considered it malpractice to admit an opinion during intermission. On the other hand, it was stuffy to make an issue of this. What he would like to do was step on Flashman's foot and disappear in the melee. He gestured noncommittally.

"These guys should stick to novels. Or maybe you don't like his novels either? I don't know what to suggest in that case. By the way, this is Belle Robinson. Belle, I'd like you to meet Max Jamison, the dean of American critics." Belle had nice lashes, but she was paralyzed in the smoke and noise, and could barely nod.

As for Flashman, he was one of the five.

"You by yourself, dean?" said Jack.

Max nodded.

"You want to go somewhere after the show? I hear there's a party over to Melman's."

"I have to get home."

"Yeah? Everything all right? How's Helen?"

Smoking should be permitted, *conversation* should not. Max was trying to concentrate on the play, hold some of its thin atmosphere down in his lungs, and here this stupid little bastard was dispersing it with his nightly small talk. Max wanted to say (but this again would be stuffy), "You're going to Melman's house and drink his booze and then go home and knock his play. Right?"

Jack Flashman led, as night to day, to Beverly Wickshire, the well-known English snot, and Felix Wye and

4

the whole slick magazine bunch. They clustered out here every first night, gossiping and introducing new girls back and forth, while the serious critics kept their own counsel. Max disliked these openings, disliked the smell and texture of the smart people, but didn't know how to protect himself yet.

He made a slow pirouette through the outer doors, and found it just as cold as he remembered; and on top of that, the same people with the same voices squirting the same blue fog. He should never have taken this job. The hell with the money. Just give me back my broom and pail. He could still see Flashman through the glass, chattering like a monkey, not a critic at all but a theater creature. Maybe Max could bypass him by sliding through the other glass door—

"Hi, Max."

Oh, Christ. He knew who that was. The jewels slipped from his lifeless fingers.

"I thought I saw you." Sam Melman, infinitely long and sad and eager. His bow tie had nearly been twisted off in ecstasies of fret. Is there anything I can do for you, thought Max. Like covering you with a sheet, or insuring your widow. He gripped Sam's hand as if to pull him to safety and Sam began shaking hands back, quite heartily. Sam was not too far gone to know that they couldn't discuss the play. They were old friends, but there were limits.

Shaking hands seemed like a good temporary solution.

"Hello, Rose. Are you nervous?"

"Uh-huh."

She looked at him with naked longing. Worse than longing, insistence. Women had no sense of fair play. As an old buddy, he would surely help Sam now, wasn't that right? She was pale and proud like a pioneer wife. She would throw old Max off the wagon when it became necessary. Max thought with his own longing of the old second-night days when nobody gave a damn about his opinions, when authors never showed up and integrity was a pleasure.

"Good luck," he said, wondering if even that wasn't compromising himself slightly, and escaped back into the theater.

"The agony recommences," said Flashman, touching his shoulder and steering him in.

Max wasn't really worried about displeasing Rose Melman. He had fought that battle long ago while no one was watching. In the back pages of *Rearview*, he had skinned several friends and acquaintances mercilessly and had braced himself for scenes—but nobody cared about *Rearview*, the bodies were cold by the time Max's column hit the stands, and scabs had formed on the playwright's wounds. "I just saw your review, Max. You're a snide bastard, aren't you?" Yes, but a snide *nonprofit* bastard, don't forget that. And are you working on anything now, George? The peaceful, innocent days, before Max Jamison became so powerful.

Sam Melman, you stink. His old chum might be a passable novelist, but he didn't know what a stage was *for*. One toilet wall fell out and that's how drama was born. Max chewed his pencil. On his new job, they liked jokes. So jokes it was. Rose, I have to see you. That's swell, Max, I just gave the dog a piece of your trouser leg. He'll recognize you anywhere. Persona non grata at the Melmans', never more to sink into those Bronx carpets, no more friends left soon. Sam, these lines, you can't mean it. If the girl comes back panting, you could maybe say, "Sam, you made the pants too long." Is *that* what they mean by jokes? Why don't you ask Mr. Stern to play "Love in Bloom," dear? Then Mr. Jamison will fall on his butt . . . And so he rattled on harmlessly, pausing to console himself that he was in better shape than Flashman, who worked for the *other* news magazine.

Flashman was not, strictly speaking, a theater critic at all, but a maid-of-all-work gossip columnist and second-string reviewer who scooped up free tickets like a mechanical crane and prowled the lobbies for carrion. If he was the only man present from his magazine, it already told you a lot about your play. The critic proper over there was a serious fellow who avoided Jack and all that Jack implied. Jack obviously didn't care. He belonged in a Broadway theater and the serious critic didn't. He was a much better judge of commercial plays, over which the serious fellow agonized to little avail. The news magazines had been toning up their operations recently with these highbrow critics, but Broadway was still Flashman's turf. He knew that you *could* give an opinion at intermission and that it would stand up. All the rest was bullshit.

Max could still hear him whispering a few seats away, going about his business, keeping the news moving like an electric fan. He was actually more intelligent than the serious fellow at his magazine (these things happened), and less corrupted by it. Max picked up the play again, reluctantly, and resumed the dreary business of accreting an opinion.

2

He typed out the Melman piece in a hurry the next morning. He meant it to be gentle, but a couple of wise-cracks darted out of his fingers and he regretfully let them lie. His masters at Now, Inc. would only allow half a column to the likes of Melman and there was no point wasting it on solemn analysis. Qualifying phrases usually went spinning to the cutting-room floor. If he had had time he would have put them in anyway, but today was an abnormally busy one.

He dropped his little bundle of gags off distastefully and kept on going to the screening room. Here he could replenish his integrity, and smoke in peace at the same time. The movie was of no special interest, but at least he could do it leisurely justice, take his time over it, punctuate as he saw fit. At *Rearview,* he had full custody of the semicolons.

The screening room was a much more congenial workshop than the *Magic Hot Box* or wherever that was last night. There were always some old friends on hand, along with the mysterious claques of relatives and hangers-on who simulated real-life conditions by laughing at the wrong times. He rolled up quietly in the elevator, wandered over lush carpets, thinking of English lawns, checked in, waved inevitably at Ferris Spender and Helga Bonbright, read the form chart, waited. None of that glamour-of-the-footlights nonsense here, but a small screen and a real ashtray.

The pleasures of the screening room were a dividend. Max had kept this much of his ass at *Rearview* mainly for reasons of honor. But he could also use the rest.

Unfortunately, the movie started. One of these new-thing, secret-agent affairs, with rockets going off at your feet and girls dressed in laminated cellophane, keeping you awake with their enormous breasts and automated rumps. The claque of relatives whooped and groaned as if it were a real movie. Perhaps it was, for all he knew.

"It is no use lamenting the new sensibility. We must learn to live with it." Hardly the tone for *Rearview.* Or anywhere else. "The new sensibility is actually at least five different sensibilities. The electronic sector, for instance, is quite distinct from the lotus land of LSD"— was that true? Sounded possible. "Naturally there are charlatans who try to package the whole deal: electronics, drop-out drugs, happenings, etc., under their own brand. Someone beginning with M. Someone else beginning with L." "Dear, how can you write about

10

LSD if you haven't taken it?" "I've read about it, talked to people. A critic doesn't have to experience everything himself." "Yes, I see."

Oh, what do *you* know? You are only a woman, Countess. "There is a common factor of impersonality in all these phenomena." All very well, Maximilian P. Jamison, but this is not getting us anywhere with this movie itself. One can't just go on laying down general principles indefinitely. Even in *Rearview*. However, he needed a language for these movies, and he hadn't got one. "An electronic aesthetic is not simply a meaningless juxtaposition of words." Isn't it though? No. Probably not. "Today's youth," oh, God, "a young person today" . . . He zoomed his prewar mind back to the picture. How did today's youthful young person keep his mind on this stuff for five minutes?—or was that the whole point?

"Traditional demands of plot and character are essentially bourgeois devices." On the other hand, they do help a fellow to concentrate. "Art is not a stewardess explaining how you inflate your life jacket"—where did *that* come from. He was pestered these days by slatternly metaphors. He considered just throwing up his hands in candid surrender. "Approving the new sensibility is one thing, finding a critical vocabulary for it is another." Some instinct, or memory, warned him off candor, for now.

The hell with the new sensibility. What he needed right now was a rest for his old one. This week brimmed over with screenings and first nights. As soon as he left here, he was due at a cocktail party for, oh, Helen Hayes. Then off to the Belasco, with a sandwich rattling around his gorge, to attend no doubt his twelfth sex comedy this month. How much entertainment should a man be asked to take?

The villain was disintegrated, from a bomb planted in his mustache, and the house lights went tentatively up. Ferris Spender struggled to his feet and said "Hi" for the second time. "How's Helen?" he asked on the way out. "O.K." "And the kids?" "They're O.K." They jogged along together to the elevator. Ferris was the kind of man who said, "Whatever became of Anna May Wong?" and meant every word of it. He had the true-blue, twelve-year-old Captain Ranger heart of a veteran film reviewer. Max had come late to movies himself (his mother believed they were bad for growing eyes, and his father that they were not art), but he liked the patter.

He walked back to the office and changed his shirt. He thought of phoning his wife, but what was the point of that? Make up your mind, snow, he spoke to his galoshes, don't just sit there. But the snow was still hovering sullenly as he walked to the other end of his small kingdom, the Commodore Hotel.

The big thing was to keep close to the canapés and away from the guest of honor. Talking to celebrities made him thirsty, and then the critical faculties got fuzzed with booze. The result could be a nightmare. He watched the waiters orbit, and stationed himself in the path of a deviled-egg man. The other guests reeked show business—this wasn't his old crowd at all, not his "theater." His people had gone to New Haven or some place. He rubbernecked a bit, idly, like a swan, it occurred to him. Flashman was talking to a well-known musical-comedy star. "What a pig," he would say later. "Hands like catchers' mitts." But he fawned on her mechanically now. For the most part the actors seemed to prefer each other's company to that of writers, while their agents pottered about trying to do a little liaison work and getting in everybody's hair.

"Hi, Max, how's Helen?"

She's all right, she's all right. No one ever asked that question in the old days, when he could have given a sensible answer. Now they were planting people at parties to nag him about it. Barbara Frye of *Woman's Work* stood around smiling.

"She doesn't like parties."

"Oh, God, sensible girl." Barbara waved her drink sadly. "And how's that fascinating little boy of yours?"

"Which one?"

"I don't know. Is there more than one?"

"Yes."

Talking about the children hurt his throat. He invented a mission across the room and left Barbara to her own devices. He would get used to these things eventually, talk of the children, etc.—talk he hadn't even taken in in the old days, for it must always have been there. Actors and actresses he had been watching for years stood between him and the bar in suburban clumps. Webster Gottschalk the agent, fussed in circles, trying to introduce people to Alison Flange, his latest creation. He spotted Max and lit up like a bow tie. Max swiveled into a hedge of stars.

He didn't want to meet these people, didn't care for actors, couldn't stand agents. He nodded severely and in a moment felt himself drifting again like a dark, hostile presence. Used—remember that?—to crash parties like this and be reluctantly excited by the show people. But now that he could come in by the front door, the show people looked like the neighbors. The actors he talked to were dull as ballplayers and degradingly anxious to please. While he was just the man from *Rearview*, they were occasionally rude to him, occasionally candid; now they all treated him like Reverend Mother.

He didn't like their damn faces and their damn clothes. He was, he realized, in a very ugly mood. Charming children, wheeling their careers like tricycles. Another tawdry old bag of a metaphor winked at him. As theater critic for *Now*, he was now a branch of show business himself; that was why he was so desperate.

Max left the party early, closing the door on a dull roar of ego. There wasn't time for a full-dress meal, so he had a moody sandwich at the Green Angel, and tried to sort out the afternoon's movie. He was stuck with an astounding memory, and could summon up every frame at will. Didn't know what to do when they arrived, though. The movie defied his kind of comment. All those years reading Eisenstein . . . he had always wanted to review movies, but for ten years the job at *Rearview* had been blocked off by Jackson Kline and Max had been left in the theater. Then one of those languid shuffles had occurred. Jackson had been bought off by *Mode;* Max, who had already gone to *Now*, in circumstances he would rather not go into, saw this as a golden opportunity to salvage his soul. Serious work for *Rearview*, trash for *Now*. He applied for Jackson's old job, at a token salary, and sat back tolerably pleased with himself. "I haven't sold out," he told Helen and the others. "I'd do it for nothing, but Biggs insists on paying at least carfare." . . . Helen's answer. His answer to her answer. And so on.

Anyhow, he had got round to movies too late, they weren't making them any more. He found himself thinking instead of his son, Justin; Barbara Frye's remark had a long fuse. Your fascinating little boy. Charlie, the baby, he could still think about fairly calmly. Placid, hard-nosed (if you could use that word of babies), relatively invulnerable, as these things go. But Justin was made of glass. His face was the most responsive Max had ever seen. His face? his whole body, you mean. Disappointments showed in his shoulders, his knees, the hang of his arms. Pleasure even more so—but pleasure made you apprehensive, because you had to make it last, and you knew you couldn't. Life could not be kept good enough for this boy.

Max knew he was being sentimental now, over his pastrami and pumpernickel. The boy wasn't that fragile. He liked to fight and all that. He would do all right. I would probably ruin him eventually with love and apprehension. The fragility is mine, not his.

Back to work. Max put on his overcoat and trudged out into thin dinner-hour snow. His heart was heavy. There was no shaking it. Life would never be quite right again, never quite what he'd hoped. It wasn't a great sorrow, but it was an authentic small one.

The play bored him even before it started. The business of having to sit on your overcoat annoyed him (either that or queue far into the night to get it out of the checkroom). And why were all these people so excited? Didn't they know that Broadway was dying of foot and mouth? Had they no decency?

Max strove to sweep and clean his mind in order to receive humble visitor. *The Family Tree* might, in defiance of the augurs in Boston, be the first good play of its kind in years; triumphing over its squint and its harelip. Being a critic, even for *Now,* meant staying alert for this, keeping the lighthouse open.

Please, not another piece on the role of the critic. It was an occupational disease, defining and redefining one's role. But he wasn't in the mood for it tonight. He wanted simply to exorcise his son from his mind, so as not to saddle the wretched play with extraneous lead weights of memory and regret. He read the program, filling himself up with past performances. Natalie Ridgeway has appeared in over two hundred television shows, poor dear. Summer stock, road companies, great mountains of experience, even in the bit parts: yet half the cast would show no trace of it, would move like truck drivers and talk like grocers.

The curtain bored him, the scenery bored him. But then, as good luck would have it, the play was incontrovertibly lousy. He didn't have to struggle. The mother alone was unbelievable. And she wasn't alone. Nobody behaved like that. You mean nobody in New York behaves like that? No, I mean nobody anywhere behaves like that. Oh, how can you be so dogmatic . . . He tried to keep these little wildcat debates to a minimum, but the play had led him right into this one. It had no claims whatever beyond a certain folksy veracity. So— was it true to life or wasn't it?

Yes, all right, he didn't get out of New York much these days, except on carefully controlled trips to university campuses. Nor, even in New York, did he sample all the humanity that was going. Who, with the freedom to choose, would spend his time with businessmen, for instance, or with women who couldn't follow jokes? It wasn't snobbery, it was simple avoidance of pain. One got enough of that in the theater.

Yes, but then don't talk about things being true to life. If you don't know anything about life, and consort only with delicate replicas of yourself—his last years with Helen, being beaten methodically with a wet sock, had left their mark on his scalp. He turned his mind to the play: trying to decide whether the mother was meant to be a convention, or just an old fart.

3

Back in his new apartment, Max consoled himself with ritual: winding the watch and clock; hanging the pants in the press; taking, as an English novelist might say, the bath. Subject for thesis: are critics neater than other people? Gottlieb and Finsterwald, neat. Bartlett and Worthing, neat with exceptions. Jamison, very neat for a non-Teuton. The question of how one felt need not be asked at all. Thinking is all in the mind.

He put on his bathrobe and went looking for a book, only to realize that the shelves were still empty. He would have to slip out next week and fetch a few cartons of books. He even thought of shining his shoes. An apartment without books was intolerable. The typewriter was the only narcotic available, and he didn't want to write any more reviews today. He had done Melman plus a tender little Scotch thing called *My Delight* this morning and he didn't want to turn into a reviewing machine.

The difference between a critic and a reviewer is, I forget. At twelve o'clock, Helen goes in to check that Justin and Charlie are covered. Pulling the blanket over hunched shoulders. God, a child sleeping. Max decided to make a drink and review his notes. Even with such uniquely average tripe as *The Family Tree*, it was important to get everything in order, a map and a dossier. He wouldn't use all that he knew, but it had to be there. Somehow, it kept one from sounding shrill.

I've always wanted to be a critic. Yes, really. Like wanting to be a dentist or an undertaker. Some kids are funny that way. No, ma'am, I have never wanted to write creatively. I was an unnatural little boy in many ways. The rumor that I used to torture flies probably contains some truth. I did write a poem once, in alexandrines, but I didn't much care for it. Yes, it's in my wallet now.

He lay on the bed and rested the drink on his chest. Shut his eyes and faded in on a screening room, where he appeared to be squeezing cellophane in his hand, and coughing at the credits. *The Max Jamison Story*, the saga of a critic. A shot rings out and blood comes streaking down his cheekbone. The eyeball is severed. Perhaps that will bring him to his senses. Helen stands in the doorway, fingering her pearl-handled revolver.

Helen had been thrilled to marry a critic. Don't tell her that now, of course. She used to attend his classes at the New School and look as if she wanted to erase his blackboard and carry his books—an attitude that both pleased and disgusted him. Her legs were very distracting but they were safer to look at than her face, until he came to know them by heart and their movement told him as much as her face; at which point there was no place to look. His divorce was still fresh and moist, and he was resolved never to marry another student. However, a man breaks down under admiration and he decided to take her out just once, if only to get to the bottom of those legs.

They went to the theater and afterwards she listened as charmingly as any girl ever had to his dissection of the play. She didn't complain about his surgical cruelty, but seemed, if anything, excited by it. As a middle-class girl, she was used to understatement followed at once by qualification: the only passion in her family being a nonstop concern for people's feelings. Her parents would have hesitated to criticize Mickey Mouse (you haven't heard *his* side). She squirmed with pleasure when Max referred to some famous director as a stupid little fag. This was the form her emancipation took.

Afterwards they went up to her apartment and, still breathing hard from the climb, made love. There was no diplomatic maneuvering. He was the master, she was the pupil. He found himself wondering, as his mouth sank into her breast, whether this was a true human encounter: saw the humor of putting it like that and bent to his task without further analysis. A few minutes later, he had that old feeling of being engulfed triumphantly —look, I've captured the professor—but that was just his old marriage acting up. Helen wasn't like that. She was still deferential, anxious to please, but without clothes their social differences were leveled quite a piece. He sensed that she had the one way of making love for everyone, from president to bat boy.

"What are you thinking?" Oh well, no one is perfect. They all asked it eventually. "I'd hate to think you were assigning me a grade," she said. Words that lingered over the years.

He laughed. "Criticism stops here. I'm just a humble performer myself at this point." They laughed together and flattered each other. In truth, he had enormous sexual pride and graded himself well. Sex was a game of morale. Ninety percent of it was pitching, as Connie Mack used to say. His mind drifted. What was he thinking, indeed.

This particular memory seemed now to be arousing him unseasonably. He shuffled his robe. *The Max Jamison Story* would never win Hollywood Code approval at this rate. The scene was only interesting in its ironies anyway. He thought of calling Susan Cram for instant relief. But that was no way to promote human encounter. He couldn't stand Susan either aurally or optically: he would have to shut his eyes and clap a hand over her mouth while making her. Fine lot of I-thou would come of that.

Anyway, to get back to the script, he found himself wanting much more of Helen after that first night. Methodically he began to fall in love. Montage of restaurants. She didn't smoke between courses. She never said anything boozily stupid at the end of the meal to unthread the whole conversation. Her physical movements were unfailingly graceful; nothing to get on the nerves there. His friends liked her. This list of necessities was no accident: his first wife had violated every one of them, in less than two years of marriage. His first wife had made a *real* critic of him.

And so the affair burgeoned against his better judgment. The banalities of the teacher-student relationship were easy to take from such a bright student. Even her scatter-gun English improved under gentle correction. She started out with the usual bleak mixture of bad folk-speech and assorted jargon—well, you can't call that stuff folk-speech, can you? Mass media-pidgin is more like it. He didn't want to get sidetracked onto that, though. Again it was interesting in the ironies.

At the end of the season, they took a summer cottage in Maine. Solitude was the sternest test. Knowing when to leave him alone. Actually reading, and not faking it. He knew that his tests were priggish, but his skin had been rubbed raw and he couldn't stand another mistake. He would snap if he heard one more literary opinion based on the review in *Time*.

There are no fool-proof tests, of course. He was unwittingly playing to her strength. She was admirable at summers—still was, for that matter. The beach bored her, quite properly. She liked walking, but didn't go on about it. She knew the names of trees. Max hated people who didn't *know* anything. Conversation with his first wife was a constant stammer, a vague gesture. She seemed always to have forgotten her notes.

It was fatally easy to get sidetracked onto summers, too. E.g., later, pregnant with Justin: he rather liked pregnant women, slopping about regally. (Helen said, oh much much later, that he liked the feeling of "Look what I've done," but by then she'd say anything.) Then, magically, Justin born and crawling the sands in bleary wonder. The right use for a beach. But by then things were not so good with Helen. So you never had everything at once.

Misery was sometimes made better by thinking about it, after all. Then at least you had a chance to get bored with it. *"The Max Jamison Story* failed to grip this viewer. Frankly, I found the point eluding me again and again. The central character is miscast. Critics should be on the small side, with fine, malicious features. Nobody is going to accept a critic of six feet two and a face like an English police sergeant. Thinning hair might be all right but not for Christsake in lank black strands, plastered from left to right. This man is clearly in the wrong movie. Inquire into butler parts.

"The girls also seem to be in the wrong order. The first wife is the doll with the steadfast qualities. Maybe the girls should have reversed roles. The second one, this Helen, makes a lousy note to finish on. Her motivation will mean nothing out of town. You simply don't break up your marriage because you don't like a man's expression. Not in Nebraska, you don't."

"Thank you very much, Mr. Flashman, for that very fine gut reaction. Now for the highbrows we bring you Max Jamison. Mr. Jamison, won't you tell our ladies what you think of the movie?"

"Well, it's very old-fashioned of course. The dialogue is quite banal and more than a little unbelievable, especially from supposedly intelligent people. The sex is tawdry and repetitive. I really think this is more Mr. Flashman's movie than mine."

—"You never rest, do you, Max? Never stop working."

That's true, not true, don't know. He took the drink off his chest and finished it: took the glass out to the kitchen, washed it and dried it, feeling for a moment like a priest. Jamison might just make it as an Anglican bishop.

He reached again for a nonexistent book. Failing that, he went back to bed and snapped off the light; he lay in the dark, *imagining* print, until he fell asleep.

4

Saturday was devoted to Justin (there wasn't as yet much point in devoting it to Charlie, whose idea of a good time was thrusting his finger through smoke rings indefinitely). For Justin, there was the circus and the ice show, in season, and homogenized Disney movies the rest of the year. Justin smelled of popcorn; it was ground into his pores by now. His T-shirt was streaked with chocolate. Max knew it was misguided, but he would make these food offerings all afternoon, so that Justin probably wouldn't eat his dinner when he got home.

Max was not naturally good with children. He tended to overrate their powers of concentration, didn't understand the stop-go quality of their intelligence. As he jogged downtown with Justin on the Fifth Avenue bus, he was tempted to discuss the affairs of the week, the state of the theater, the mess in Washington. Justin looked out the window tactfully.

"How was school this week?"

"All right."

"What did you learn?"

Justin shrugged. Learn? School? There must be some mistake.

"Did you do arithmetic?"

Justin nodded.

"Spelling?" You can't see anything through that window, Justin. It's got a sticker on it. Look at me, please. Max wanted to put his arm on the boy's shoulder, but felt awkward about it. It would be theatrical and pointless. Children didn't seem to mind being touched, or even notice it. It was strange.

There was no conversation for twenty slow blocks, for which Max took full responsibility. He loved being with Justin, but their dialogue was severed in too many places. They were always in an outing situation now, always dressed up, traveling, looking for food and men's rooms. A separated father automatically became an uncle. Was Justin possibly a little bit nervous with him? He pictured his own big, severe face as it must look to the boy—supposing a face proportionately bigger than his own was looking down at *him*? A huge demi-urge peering through the bus window.

"Guess what, Dad?" Justin suddenly came to life. "Murray just got a new bicycle. Can I have one too?"

"Can you ride one?"

"Sure, I can."

"Well, I guess so. Where do you ride in the city?"

"In the Park, of course."

Let me give you a bicycle and a car and a basketball. Let me festoon you with gifts. Please accept them, please. But Justin just wanted the bicycle for now. He said, "Murray's got a new girlfriend."

"He has? Isn't he a little bit young for that?"

"He's seven."

"Oh, that's all right then."

Lucky Murray. Maybe Murray's girl has a friend for Max. Max was undoubtedly getting raunchy and anti-social. Girls in buses pulled their skirts down when old Max came aboard. Must do something about that soon, before the papers hear about it.

"How about you, Justin? Have you got a girlfriend?"

"Oh, sure. Same old one—Ruby."

Jewish, eh? Everyone's Jewish these days. She'll give Justin smart kids, right, Mama? The thought of a girl-friend at seven did not really amuse Max. It was one of those awful jokes from the forties. Helen, of course, was all for it. She would, under pressure, say that it was healthier than the way Max was brought up. Who's to say?

They got out at Fiftieth and began walking cross-town. Justin, very serene and self-contained. Now don't, for pitysake, turn into a teenager. We'll go away some-where instead . . . Already, Justin's hair was longer than Max liked. What's wrong with long hair? Well, nothing of course. But in our society it is a symbol of sexual identification, and we can't have too many of those, can we? But that's arbitrary, Max, it's tribal. Yes, dear, but what isn't? Just because something is tribal doesn't mean it is unimportant. You think that under-neath all the tribal layers you're going to find the real man. Well, let me tell you something, baby, there isn't anything under the overcoat at all. Not so much as a six-inch dwarf. What a burner on you, dumpling. The over-coat is the man.

Arguments that began "in our society" always turned out badly. Anyhow, he had lost the long-hair argument, because Justin wouldn't go to the barber, and Helen wielded the scissors at home. Helen would probably do some terrible things to Justin before she was through.

As luck would have it, the afternoon's movie featured a teenage singing group to massage his fixation: four pasty-faced yahoos with hair streaming down their backs, smashing your eardrums with every device of science—sorry, I just don't like this stuff. That's because you're uptight. You're an old man. You're as good as dead. A great, rusty corpse, propped up in plaster band-ages, laying down the Mosaic law. You have no business reviewing these things at all. It isn't fair to turn a dead old man loose on a bunch of kids.

Justin chewed softly, jiggling slightly but otherwise taking things quietly. Did this mean the age of scream-ers was about to end? Was all this banging and moaning to be received henceforth with small cool smiles and a twitching of sneakers? He decided to delve into the concept of cool for a spell, and so passed the balance of the movie without ill effect.

Justin asked for a hotdog as soon as they got outside, and the moment his hands were on it, flashed ketchup obscenely along its flank. Things might have been worse, he might have asked for pizza. Max felt a rush of hopeless, muddled tenderness as he watched Justin eat. When you saw your kids only at intervals, you were lopsided with sentimentality. You sometimes even felt like crying. Max the rat, lord high executioner, crying over his children. He doesn't *like* them, he doesn't *know* them, he just weeps over them. Like Hitler weeping over a dead cat.

Oh, Christ! not *that* argument. He paid the man before Justin could start talking sundae. They walked back to the bus, Justin mooning and scratching.

"So how did you like the movie, Justin?"

"It was neat."

"Which part did you like especially?"

"The part where the guy fell down."

When they got home, Justin, son of critic, would give a breathless, incoherent rundown. And it would end "And then this guy fell down," as if that had been the whole point of the movie. As the winter evening closed in, the sentimentality overwhelmed Max, filling his lungs like water. He couldn't just walk out and leave Justin for a whole week. He would sit on the sofa and refuse to move.

Let's hope Helen won't be in yet. He would slip Charlie a couple of smoke rings and make his getaway. Helen's unmarried sister Beth was staying in the apartment. Helen was out shopping in the slush some place. Little plaid sportshirts from Bloomingdale's. A question of taste. There was a stack of mail out on the doormat, mostly for him—screenings, word of the latest happenings, copious word of Sandra Dee and Tuesday Weld, beginning shooting in Acapulco, finding role a gweat big challenge, based on Hugo Pomfret's best-selling novel—

Max leafed through the crud while waiting for Beth to open the door. Some mimeograph machines never caught up with you, they sent news releases to the place of your birth. The doormen, that was another problem, laid out the mail whenever it suited them these days. Five o'clock on a Saturday afternoon probably struck them as an elegant time to deliver mail. The country might be swinging on the surface, but underneath it was stiff and sluggish, barely able to make the basic moves or keep things going. Max pressed the button again, fiercely. He had handed over his key two weeks ago and was reduced to this.

Such a manly prod should produce something more satisfying than those goddamn chimes. He was about to really belt it when he heard a quick step behind the door. His irritation had been mainly nervousness. Those feet were Helen's, and he didn't want to see Helen right now.

She was still beautiful, with her slightly Oriental eyes and black bangs, and he registered it automatically. The skin would last forever. The hands were those of a child. She was staring back wryly, as if to say, "I'm not a prize Angus, that isn't the way to look at women, you know." He turned aside quickly and steered Justin toward her. She smiled, not in a bad mood at all. Of course, bad moods weren't ever the real problem, just the rocket fuel.

"How was the movie?" she asked.

"It was crazy. This guy was running down the street and there was this big fruit thing, you know, melons and stuff." Max winced at the crash that was to come.

"And this monkey that had escaped was leaning over the balcony of Mr. Foxberry's town house . . ."

Max stood awkwardly in the foyer, not sure whether to advance or retreat. It was typical of Justin to remember the phrase "town house." The kid had a pedantic streak, a gift from father. Helen stood smiling at Justin's rigamarole. Max was sorely tempted to give his own version of the plot and get it over with. Meanwhile, question: "Do insipid movies impair immature brains?" So much of life insipid anyway, so what's the harm? Besides, they see a whole different movie than we do—from we do—from which we do. They see the people running and falling, that's all they see. You notice he doesn't mention that there was singing: imagine the joy of not noticing that! A man could die of rheumatism out here in the hall . . .

Helen helped Justin off with his rubbers and they went stomping into the apartment. Although it was on the East Side it looked as if it belonged on the West Side: endless corridor with peeling green paint; high, dim ceilings; and a poor-but-proud john with a chain dangling from the light bulb. The Jamisons could afford a better place than this—but now that they could, they didn't want it. Charlie was waiting for him in the living room, but then turned his back and ran and stuck his head in the sofa cushions. Helen was talking. The voice scratched at his ears. He had loved the voice more than anything: cool for outdoors and for asking questions in class, warm for in bed and such. The voice of a self-made "lady," one of Henry James' brave American girls. Even when the voice had ceased being used for peace-

ful purposes, it continued to enchant him: which set up
an intolerable tension. He wished now that she would
shut up. He would get out of here with no further
trouble if she would just shut up.

He tried, listlessly, to frolic with Charlie. But Charlie
was down on him today, surly and bristling with suspi-
cions. What are *you* doing here? In my mother's house?
Children could be brutal, couldn't they? Helen was asking Justin what he wanted for supper. And Justin,
stuffed with movie-house effluvia, was saying he didn't
want any supper. "I bought him a hotdog," said Max. "A
hotdog?" What kind of supper is that? None of your
business, Miss . . . Miss . . . I didn't catch your
name. You seem to forget, *I'm* the teacher.

He kept trying to play with Charlie, picking up the
wax phone and pretending to speak to him. Answer
your damn phone, kid. Charlie turned his back and
stared at the sofa frill. Helen is systematically freezing
me out. Out of my own house. The kids won't look at
me, they're afraid they'll turn to snow. Little lumps of
coal for eyes, just like their mother. My God, if she
doesn't stop talking.

She had her back to him as if some extempore boycott
was in the works. Nothing intentional of course. But
Max found himself speculating what length of blunt instrument it would take to reach the top of her skull, and
how hard the blow would have to be. He couldn't kill
her in front of the kids of course. Maybe he could get
them out of the house on some ruse.

Max wasn't joking. He had come close to killing
Helen at least once and might do it again. He started for
the door. That woman drove him absolutely crazy. If he

were to strike her once, he would do so again and again; and the children would fly at his trouser legs like whippets and hang there for dear life, shrieking and cursing. Not a wild fantasy, but sober truth.

He waved a kiss at Charlie. Justin came over for personalized treatment. "Good night, Max," said Helen lightly. Good night, you bitch. Just because you didn't say anything unpleasant for once . . . He let himself out. Critics don't really kill people. They don't have to. As for Justin, Max would try not to think of him for the next hour or so. After that, it usually wasn't so bad.

5

He was quite shaken by this wanton splurge of anger and ducked into Vincent's, the old family saloon, to quiet himself. Once upon a time, practically nothing had made him angry; then slowly and patiently, Helen had learned the ways to do it. By now, his responses were so keen that she didn't need to use her techniques any more; her face and voice set him off automatically, and even the way she arranged the furniture. His spleen, if it were, say, photographed by *Life* magazine, would look like Coney Island in mid-season.

Seamus the bartender gave him a fat greeting. Vincent's was the scene of many of Max's first experiments in loathing. He and Helen would pull in for a nightcap,

in a fairly neutral mood. Then, while Seamus diddled
with the radio, hunting for soupy ballads to hum, Helen
would methodically whip her husband into an insensate
rage.

Her tolerant, *human* tone of voice.

"You have a theory about everything, don't you,
Max?"

If Seamus was going to go on singing "Galway Bay,"
why the hell didn't he learn the words. During all those
years while things were going from bad to worse, Seamus never got past "And watch the sun go down on Galway Bay."

"Theories, but no beliefs. No position."

"I believe in standards. People should learn the words
of songs, for instance. Seamus is a disgrace to his
people."

The Story of a Marriage, by Baron von Clausewitz.
"Just a critic, only a critic. What kind of life is that?"
"You thought it was splendid once." "Yes, but I never
thought it would stop here." "You said, and I quote, 'All
these people who want to create, and they aren't half as
creative as you are.'" "You wanted me to say that. I was
the pupil." "I don't consider criticism an end in itself."
"Oh yes, you do. You love it. You love being teacher.
You" etc., etc. Married people shouldn't be allowed to
drink together, not after the first two years. All the
erotic energy plowed into this kind of thing. Death
play.

Max got up, prying himself from the sticky red
leather, and went over to the jukebox. There were real
Gaelic songs on it. He would silence Seamus with these,

and possibly shame him too. To be honest, Max did not especially like Irish songs, all those jigs and dirges, but one might as well have the real thing.

When they got back from their summer cottage, they were as good as married. And in the fall they made it official, in St. Wilbert's Episcopal Church. (They agreed that registry offices were tacky.) The theater season was just beginning to coagulate and Helen was still excited about going to the second nights. He dismantled the plays for her afterwards, as before, and then, in intellectual heat, made love.

"I thought I liked this play, until you told me why I didn't."

"That's what I'm for."

"O.K., but don't tell me during the intermission, will you, Max? You keep ruining second acts."

Max agreed. He had fallen into the bad habit of formulating his wisecracks, and hence his opinions, prematurely. Even on a little magazine, you could fall into sleazy ways. Helen preached fairness. She frowned on glibness. All good things that she did for him.

Young marriage in New York. Max had done renovated brownstones last time, and you can't go the quaint route more than once. He was beyond the stage of bumping up stairs with bags of laundry. His combined income, age thirty-six at that point, had won him an elevator of sorts, big enough to cart antique chairs, one of his weaknesses in those days. Helen, marrying for the first time, was obliged to forgo the night at the Plaza, the decision to decorate Chinese. Not that she seemed to mind.

He doggedly went on reviewing, getting better, he thought, in a field where improvement is seldom noticed. He had been doing it since college and felt that he was only just getting on top of it, moving in rhythm with the work instead of against it. Looking back, he saw that as a rather freakish period when things went naturally that aren't supposed to go naturally: a brainless, athletic period. People talked of old Max mellowing. He praised a few more dogs than usual out of an excess of responsiveness. His motto for that brief spell was: Better to err on the side of indulgence than to miss a masterpiece.

Happiness comes to the critic. An unnatural condition indeed. Of course, it was only a slight modulation. To the untrained eye, he was still a bastard. "Believe me, darling," he told Helen, "I'm much nicer than I used to be." She was not as thrilled by his war games as she used to be. Suddenly, a Thursday in February or a Monday in March, she changed on that. She said, lightly, what all the others said. "Don't you *like* the theater? Yes, yes, I know. Standards." "I love the theater. You know that." "I know, that's why it makes you so wretched, isn't it?" Her emancipation undone, she had gone back to being charitable. The American vice. The poison arrives, first, affectionately. She fondled him while she said these stupid, tiresome things. Next time, she would dispense with that.

But his nastiness wasn't the real problem. He could always cut down on that, at least in conversation. He wasn't really a bastard, it was just a professional habit, a kind of shorthand. Believe me, there is nothing personal. Does the surgeon hate the stomach? Well, yes, probably. He has every reason to. Max stretched out his glass to Seamus. He had meant to pick up some books tonight, damnit. With neither books nor viewings, sightings, soundings, to occupy him he might as well have another drink: brood about the parties he hadn't been invited to, the action he was missing thanks to somebody's malice . . .

No, the chief *numero uno* problem was not his nastiness. (A lesser man would be saying this to the bartender, but Max thought he made a brighter audience himself.) It was, well, by the second year, Helen said again what they all say: "Is this all?" Again, with love, the same sneaky gestures. This time he got peeved: a whole year's instruction unstitched. "Is this *all?* Isn't this *enough?*" It was infuriating because he had explained, and she had ardently agreed, that criticism was one of the very few honorable professions open to a man. She couldn't want to hear all that again? God, he hated stupidity.

"I know," she said, wheedling her hand along his leg. "It's just that, by itself, there's something—arid."

Ever so timid about it, easily beaten back by his savage counterattack. Arid! The variety of the work, the creativeness, the part you play in nursing and pruning the nation's talent. And then, the possibility, never fully achieved, of making literature of your own work. Sainte-Beuve, Matthew Arnold, Bernard Shaw, Stark Young, zzzzzz. Yes, dear, of course, dear. Nothing arid about Stark Young. He made love with vicious authority, clinching his point. Or so he thought.

It was only some time later that he realized that she was working on the assumption that *she* had won the point. It was hard to describe. This attitude—a kind of "Oh yes, Max: he's still doing his criticism, you know." As a woman might admit that her husband snored. Helen always decided for herself whether she had won an argument: never mind what the scoreboard said.

He thought, for a mad instant, of countering with a novel of his own, some earnest bit of trash that would raise his status to that of "writer." But he understood the fraudulence of that. He must just go on being himself. She was bored with his written criticism now. After reading several miles of it, she had just given up—fair enough; it was his vocation, not hers. He called her attention to essays he was especially pleased with and she left them lying around the kitchen. He reproached himself for having expected anything else, for expecting or wanting the master-student bit to last forever.

A critic doesn't have to be happy, that isn't one of his categories. Max had become, by elimination, dean of the little magazines, just as his wife was losing interest. Most of his rivals gave up one by one and hitched themselves to universities or foundations. That was the normal thing. Broadway was worth no man's whole lifetime. "Max, how can you stand it, year after year," said Waldo Funk, on a royal visit from Stanford. I can't, Waldo, but I must. Bad times must be endured. His colleagues left him and new ones sprouted up: saying in falsetto how bored they already were with the Broadway stage. Using the dead horse to advance themselves.

He seldom went to the *Rearview* office, because no one ever seemed to be there. The magazine had changed hands, the staff had been re-upholstered. What they thought of him, he hardly knew. His life had a proper hermit-like quality. He and Helen went to parties, but belonged to no set. A fierce independence was an essential precondition, like the spotless white nightgown that Balzac used to write in. Max, entering his cave, screwing in the jeweler's glass, turning the gems over in his fingers. Couldn't Helen see the beauty and delicacy of this?

"Max, we're not getting anywhere."

"Where do you want to get?"

"Everything is so tentative. No real friendships, no real *aim* . . ." Essay: Americans have to be getting somewhere. Oblivion races just behind them. Ah yes, and how is it in *your* country, M. Pamplemousse? Max wanted no more from life than he had had at that moment—that and the peace to polish his craft. She had sworn she understood that, still swore for that matter. But she had in her Midwestern bones this belief in motion. No matter how good it was where you were, you must keep going: a fellowship at Brandeis, head of the drama school at Montana U., onward and upward, onward *was* upward, something new to tell people every season. "Joe just got promoted, we're going abroad for a year, research grant, presidential sub-committee." Meanwhile, the crazy old monk works away in his cave, scrutinizing, frowning, laying aside.

At what point did *he* begin to question what he was doing? A pretty question. But let's stick to the sequence here. We have now been married for three years, and Helen has practically stopped going to the theater. This is pretty funny, because she always accused me of beating up on plays and not enjoying them enough. But now I go and she doesn't. Instead, she becomes pregnant.

Motion, change, will be served that way. We don't even have to change apartments, we will redecorate hell out of this one.

There are parts of the apartment that nothing can be done for, that damn hallway, for instance—too narrow for people to see what's on the walls—or the toilet, which is just big enough for one funny picture. (We fight mildly about that: I detest funny pictures in johns. She says, If you had your way, everyone would wear a black suit and tie. Some justice in that, I suppose, but beside the point.) But whatever can be changed is. Under cover of pregnancy, she modernizes the living room: O.K., she has good taste, it works. My taste should not be allowed to dominate indefinitely. I was the one who wanted to liquidate the master-pupil thing, remember? She turns the study into a nursery.

She was rather sweet and absent-minded at that time, with a tendency to share jokes and collapse against him. There was nothing mutinous going on, just preparations for a mutiny. Thus when all was in readiness, and the baby—new super-weapon—was installed, she could say, bright and cold, "I've done something, what have *you* done?" Still plodding to the theater through snow-drifts and gnawing my finger at the typewriter, lining up little opinions like mud pies.

Babies are real. Things like an interest in literature are games that you then put aside. One must be prepared for that with some women. But it was worse than that in this case. Quite simply and from the moment she came back from the hospital, Helen despised him; or his career, which was the same thing. It was not fit work for the father of her child.

He got up from the bar. That was enough analysis for one day. Solitude must be rationed. Another drink would turn it into a threshing nightmare. How can she say I'm cool, unemotional—look at me now, gentlemen. His body suddenly ached with frustration. It must show . . . oh yes, you can feel sorry for yourself, Max. *That* emotion you can manage—your party trick. Very powerfully and impressively sorry for yourself. Crying over your own performance, like Hitler at Götterdämmerung.

Whether or not she was right, he must stay cool for now. A sorrowful bleat on the telephone would never do. He would like most of all to go to a party, any party. The Godwins were having a small one later. He might go there and show off. He needed his mead of praise for the day. Meanwhile, to stay cool, there was always Susan Cram. Susan, sex for sex's sake, he despised that. Yet, without it, he felt weak and unsure of himself.

He balanced on his palm the pros and cons. "Look at your father." His family silently watching while he humped Susan. Watch the critic, in a fabulous display of taste. Listen to the master of language. "Susan, darling Susan, pet." Well, one had to say something.

Pretty heavy, that side of the ledger. But, on the other, impotence and self-pity, weakness, fear of offending (yes, it can happen to anyone, even a Jamison) and the final disgrace: the writing of ingratiating reviews. God knows, he hadn't asked for this problem. He could, if he wished, be out seducing teeny-boppers or minor actresses. I can get your statistics in *Now*, baby. Susan was better than that. Susan was nothing.

He strolled over to the wall telephone. In strict fact,

his family would not be watching him. Maybe soon he could work out something a little more impressive. But sex in New York was an ailing form, like, oh, theater in New Jersey, or opera in the Philippines, and an artist can only work with what's there.

6

In that frame of mind, it was always hopeless. Discharging his seed into Susan was like planting it among rocks. No peerless Justin would result from it, but only another of Susan's abortions if all went wrong; or, if she got idealistic for once, a listless fag, a fat little nothing with Mother's brain and Critic's lousy attitude. As he lay on top of Susan, taking in her vacuous whimpers and stereotyped writhings, he decided that this must certainly be the last time. Even before the end, he was raging at himself and punishing her.

When will I see you again, Max? A friend gave me these tickets, we could go driving—she always had a little picnic basket of plans for him afterwards.

He ate a hamburger with her while she laid them out

carefully. Susan always acted as if they were real lovers, who were kept apart only by a series of monstrous inconveniences. It was up to him to provide a fresh crop of these every time.

"I've been reading your reviews in *Now*," she said, after the regretful rejections were done.

"Oh yes?"

She nodded, and waited for him to ask what she thought of them. Praise from her was not exactly what he had in mind. It would even hurt slightly. Still, it was better than nothing.

"What did you think?"

"Well—" She stirred her coffee ominously.

"Well what?" he asked impatiently.

"Well—it must be frustrating for you, after *Rearview*."

"What do you mean by that?"

"You could write what you wanted there, couldn't you? At *Now*—it's very good of course, what you're doing there, but I feel . . ."

Oh God, the things that vanity got you into. He almost laughed. Susan's praise meant nothing; you wouldn't ask for it if there was any chance of not getting it. Yet her disapproval stung.

"I blame it on our economic system. That a man like you has to work for a magazine like that . . ."

Or sleep with a woman like you, he thought. The pale eager flesh peered through the housecoat at knee and breast. Dressed or undressed, it made no difference to Susan. She probably had to look to see which she was. I happen to think I'm doing quite well at *Now*, I haven't sold out. But you don't waste time bargaining for Su-

45

san's esteem. You have just heard what everybody else is saying, a lot more gently than they're saying it. You may change Susan, but you can't change *them.*

He felt for a moment petty and quarrelsome. The way a woman sits tells you the way she thinks. Susan, I judge from the way your legs spraddle that you are stupid, helplessly, gallantly stupid. I apologize for taking your time.

He kissed her on the mouth and waved off another shower of plans. Maybe he could recoup at the Godwins'. He was angry, wanted to defend himself at the last ditch. *It is brainless snobbery to think that working for a news magazine is automatically a sell-out.* Please pass that on to all your dumb friends.

Where had he picked up this recurrent need for praise? It was usually a sign of old age, so much he knew from observation. When he was younger, he had despised it like everybody else, without understanding its special charms. It had, he believed, something to do with boredom. And something to do with his line of work—always a second banana, never a bride. Then also the certainty that people were assembling outside in the dark, murmuring angrily. But mostly, mostly, it was the wounds of war with his wife; the war that he still refought in his head like a shell-shocked veteran, making up battles that never happened, and adding them to the screaming, whining truth. Everyone who didn't like him was running guns to his wife; everyone from whom a compliment could be extracted was at least neutral.

• • •

He got medium-drunk at the Godwins', to round off his Saturday. Fornication, booze, and flattery—these were not enough, he still insisted, but they were enough for Saturday night.

"How was *Burned-out Dawn?*"

"Terrible."

"I was afraid of that. Wendell Stead liked it."

"Yes, well, there you are. Stead is the test. Did you know that Wendell talks in his sleep? I heard him once in the intermission. He was saying that he thought it would be nice if Samuel Beckett would use his very real God-given talent to say something positive."

They laughed a little—this was not a great crowd of laughers. People who made too much of Critic's jokes made him nervous and irritable, also made him resolve to tell no more. Working in the theater taught you to hate un-toilet-trained laughter.

"Wendell keeps asking Edward Albee to write another play like *Zoo Story*. He completely forgets that he also panned *Zoo Story*." Critic in tight white pants regaling the crowd at Garrick's. "Where would we be without Wendell to pick on? However low you sink in this profession, there is Wendell gazing up at you. From the bottom of the bowl."

He went to the kitchen for ice cubes and found Edgar and Janice Godwin wrangling over some movie. Instinctively he moved in, like a house dick. A critic's work was never done. In some houses, you would find a bright kid laying for you, wanting to shoot it out. In others, like this one, his word was law. Civilization had reached Tombstone.

"What seems to be the trouble?"

"I'm telling Edgar that Antonioni's pointlessness *is* the point."

"And I'm saying, who needs such points?"

Oh God. Antonioni. Max tried to clear his head. He had a lot to say about this, but they wouldn't want the whole lecture. Edgar was looking at him red-eyed. "I seem to remember you liked the last one, Max. In fact, I thought your review was lousy."

"Edgar!"

"Well, I did. Max doesn't mind hearing things like that. He dishes it out pretty good in his own column. Right, Max?"

"That's right." Oh, oh. One of the punk gunmen. *Here.* Edgar, of all people.

"I personally think you sometimes go a little too far in that direction," Edgar bored in. "Max sometimes writes as if people had no feelings at all. Is that barely possible, Max?"

"It's possible."

"Edgar, what's gotten into you tonight?"

"Nothing. Max doesn't mind. He says worse things than that every week of his life. Some poor bastard who's given two years of his life, O.K. the result's lousy but he believes in it, and along comes Max with his butcher's knife . . ."

"I happen to think that good theater is more important than individual feelings."

"Oh, sure."

"Edgar!"

"What's the matter? I just said 'Oh, sure.'"

It was like getting a drunk out of the taxi and in the right door. The poor sonofabitch had lost his thread.

48

"Believe it or not, Edgar, I get nastier stuff in my mail every day than I ever put in my column. Critics have feelings too, you know."

"Oh, sure." Edgar turned on his heel abruptly and swaggered out, leaving Janice alone with Max. She looked at him apologetically—no, more than apologetically, tenderly. Max had a fuzzy, treacherous illumination. Edgar didn't like him. Therefore his jolly times at the Godwins' were all Janice's doing. Therefore, therefore. Better test the steps again, just to be sure. Edgar no like. Surprise. Edgar always very friendly fellow. Ah well, these things happen. Janice friendly indeed, looking at him now with big violet eyes. Therefore, a pass is in order. Right?

—Look at Daddy now, children. Stumbling from woman to woman. Not because he wants them, but because they're willing. This is the emptiness I was telling you about. Now on our right . . .

Now wait a sweet minute on that. Janice was not to be compared for one instant with Susan. Helen had got him doubting everything, had made him his own severest critic. He had always been hot for Janice, only his huge friendship for Edgar had kept it in bounds. This was not a bad thing at all. He put his arms around Janice and she whispered, "Oh Max," and he tried to believe he was onto something at last. But all he got from her was wave after wave of goofy admiration. And while he was always grateful for that, he despised the people who provided it. Admiration was menial work. Despised and distrusted them, like sneaky servants.

He stood back from her, praying for some deeper quality, now that she had declared herself. His bout with Susan had barely touched him, he wanted much more. But all he could see in her eyes was tipsy confusion, the remains of a quarrel with her husband, a crush on critics; and beyond that, a bad morning for both of them. It was better to stick with Susan.

Edgar came back after a while in a much friendlier state of mind, and Janice nuzzled him as if nothing had happened. These people were gassed. Silly children who might set fire to the house by mistake. He retrieved his coat and left, feeling rather pleased with himself over having dodged the flames. Being a critic had certain practical uses—simply no spiritual or intellectual ones.

7

Max's set-up with Helen had as yet no legal or social definition, and he spent that kind of Sunday. He didn't want a second divorce—it was like two marks on your driver's license. In fact, he didn't know precisely what he wanted. Helen was willing to wait, so long as he didn't try moving back with her. She didn't care what people thought. She wouldn't go out with him to keep up appearances, but she didn't advertise their separation unseasonably. She behaved as sensitively as one had grown to expect.

Max read the Sunday *Times* in pale sunlight. A gutted grapefruit, a bowl with cornflakes stuck to the side. A black shade that had snapped all the way up. Italian neo-realism. Max panned to Max frowning over the drama section. What manner of crap is this? Need for repertory theater. Need for home-grown actors. Crying need for cheaper tickets, shorter runs, matching grants. Wider seats, smaller actors, rotating fellowships. The new multi-million-dollar playhouse in Fort Worth will be completed in fifteen years' time.

Max liked theater talk. It was a little-known fact that he had acted once upon a time himself, even had a clipping from the Hartford *Courant* to prove it. "In a style alternately wooden and florid," it said right there. Max had also directed several college productions, and had learned to respect the simple miracle of getting the curtain up every night. Would that the miracle occurred less often, of course.

Things to do today. He couldn't take Justin out again. There was a limit to how many outings a normal boy could stand. And besides, Helen had said something about a birthday party. Justin's set had a record number of birthdays. Max's had none at all.

He thought about going to church for an hour or so. At his age, religious conversion was considered entirely appropriate. And he just had time for one right now, in his busy schedule. But he couldn't bring himself to like Christianity. Blessed are the meek was sniveling talk. He couldn't see how humility was good for people. It gave them an excuse for mediocrity, and God knows, most people didn't need one. The liturgical side was not displeasing to him, and he had the usual gamy interest in Catholic doings (nothing humble about those cardinals), but now they were mucking that up too, leaving nothing but the empty box.

Belief in a social cause then, belief in politics. Meetings, rallies, addressing envelopes. Belief in the Negro. Usually a fake. Would certainly be in his case. Could not just decide to believe in something because you wanted to, and put out your shingle like all those women who rattled when they moved. Belief in the arts was quite enough for one man.

Ah, even that— He felt he had been pressured into accepting someone else's terms. Faith was a rhetorical trick that he didn't really care to use. Or else an excuse for dropping your guard and writing badly. Intellectually crippling and terribly American. What's the alternative, Mr. Jamison? Just to take what is there, and deal with it, piece by piece: all that anyone can really do anyway. Makes no difference to God whether Max Jamison believes in Him or not. The Holy Ghost will bear me out on that, I think.

Still, faith was very attractive to women. It would have helped his marriage. When Helen joined the Reform Democrats, and when Helen supported SNCC and marched on Mississippi, and when she joined the Ladies Auxiliary for a Better World and marched all over (like Mayor La Guardia chasing fires), he felt suddenly chilly and alone, like an old man in a doorway. So he decided that he believed in Art.

Helen was not impressed by that. She was not impressed, either, by his signature protesting the war in Vietnam or even by his refusal to pay taxes. She knew the score.

"Why do you bother, Max?"

"I think it's important."

"You don't give a damn about Vietnam and you know it." How could one be sure?

"Why do you think I'm doing it then?" he asked her.

"Your sense of theater perhaps. A chance to thrust yourself in front of the war and take a bow. Passion for seeing your name on lists."

A breakfast-type argument, crude to the palate. The table strewn with peace pamphlets and civil-rights news letters. She knew that he never bothered to read them, even to please her; that he was bored with the war and bored with the Negro. She thought she knew.

"Anyone can sign things," she said. "It only takes a second."

"What about the taxes? I could go to jail for that."

"I doubt it. But what a joke that would be—you going to jail over Vietnam."

"Well, I might."

She was just silent and amused. She read her pamphlets, and he was jealous of them. She didn't read the choice bits out loud to him any more, but enjoyed them all in secret. He realized that this was why he had signed the tax thing—to elbow in among the pamphlets and become her leader again.

"Leading writers protest war—that's you," she said, looking up. "It must be fun to be a leading writer."

By that time, they both knew he couldn't win. They had reached the exhausted level of flat sarcasm and contempt, where the insults didn't have to be precise or logically airtight. Picture two shell-shocked snipers in a burned-out town, firing randomly.

"My little defects are not, believe it or not, terminal cancers," he said.

"You want to bet?" The more tragic a marriage became, the shriller and glossier the wisecracks.

A week after that one, he moved out for good.

He realized he had been scanning the drama section for his own name. "Engrossing"—*Now*, wasn't good enough. He had never used that word in his life; must be his ardent substitute, Dick Shaw. "Mature Drama"—Jack Flashman. How would you know, Jack? Max hadn't liked much this season. If he wanted to get the old name in print, he had better moisten his pen, plunge it in butter and honey.

Drama mailbag. Ho hum. The usual attacks on John Simon. Need for repertory, etc., etc. Hey, here was one. Only three serious critics left in the country: Max Jamison and—never mind the other two mountebanks. Just turn to page 19, Helen, in the *N.Y. Times!* Read all about my integrity, my standards, my merciless intelligence. Christ, somebody had noticed. Abel Morris, Westchester. *He* noticed. Bless you, Abel. Westchester is a better place for having you. Those qualities cost something, Helen. In this case, a wife and two sons. You think you can have those virtues of mine and not get a little twisted? Think you can remain a healthy American boy?

Pathetic? Certainly, he knew he was being pathetic. Swooning over some creep in Westchester. The *Times* might just as easily have printed the other letter instead, the one that accused Jamison and his school of confusing personal malice with the higher morality, and he would be proportionately cast down.

But confidence was his stock in trade, and he needed

a shot right now. You didn't require much of it to wheel out the trash, but you needed plenty when the good stuff came along. The relaxed concentration and the stamina of a brain surgeon: you couldn't do it if you were forever fussing about your credentials. You couldn't do it with a wife who questioned your right to judge the janitor's cat, who thought your whole mind and soul were based on a false premise. That, of course, accounted for his side of the break.

Closing the *Times* was the end of his religious observance for the day. He wished real religion wasn't quite so damn impossible. There was a need for it that the *Times* didn't really fill. How about a little art instead? He thumbed through the concerts, nothing grabbed him there. It was another great day for Beethoven. He felt, just for the moment, an allergy to theater seats. He would like to perch on a rock and listen to someone playing the flute. It was also a nice day to watch a cat preening on the windowsill, if he had a cat. How's about a little painting? He had heard that museums were a great place to pick up girls. Thoughtful girls that you could take home to your wife . . . He decided just like that on the Guggenheim. It would be nice to spiral down past the Klees and Kandinskys, round the hurdy-gurdy museum with its bright white walls, and girls splashed like butterflies.

He didn't really suppose he would find a girl there. Girls were something you stole from drunks at parties. There was no other way.

Yet, to his wonderment, he did find one. A beautiful

girl in front of a Gauguin that had got in by mistake. Felt suddenly like an infinitely old old man with a candy box under his arm and a fistful of crushed daisies. He stood there long enough to establish himself, and then said, "What do you think of it?" He usually allowed someone else to introduce him to his victims. This was like being arrested in some men's room. "I think it's terrible." "Why were you looking at it then?" "I was waiting for you to say something." He was on his guard right off. Was she brash and harebrained? Not to the naked eye. Was she going to say, I attended your course at Hunter last year? The danger passed.

"Well, I think it's awful too. But what can we do about it?"

"We could paint a mustache on it," she said.

She wore a miniskirt, which he didn't usually like, but didn't mind in this case. On her it seemed sensible and civilized. She looked as if she could give you accurate directions—the first thing he looked for in a woman these days. His first wife had cured him of any taste for dumbness, vagueness, helplessness: the Uncle Tom slave brand of women. Tie your own damn shoelace was his motto about that.

He sniffed closer. Watch out for girls who are too good to be true. They are concealing some enormous defect. Did she do this often? Was she a collector? Two Francis Bacons and they agreed to break for tea.

He didn't want to identify himself too soon. People were not always themselves with even mini-celebrities. It was often tempting, after a hard day, to put on one's medals ("Special citation, Prague Pavilion, 1899") and let those do the talking. But he hadn't had a hard day. He felt suddenly fresh and strong, bursting with curiosity. He would go on his less public merits.

What did she do, art student, good; she had a reason to be there, other than bagging the Furtive Lecher. Home, Connecticut (shrug—a morally neutral answer). Present abode, East Eleventh. Sorry to ask so many questions, miss, won't ask any more. Max a little rusty at this. The New Girl is supposed to be different from her mother. One heard rumors. "Striding along freely, unfettered by convention, or excessive clothing, frankly interested in sex" . . . better forget all that crap, and follow the old firehouse bell.

"Are you doing anything this evening?"

"Yes, I am."

"Oh, you are?"

"Uh-huh. Yes. I am."

"Washing out socks, or catching up on your correspondence?"

"No—a real date."

The old man with the daisies never got past the concierge. Actually, Max didn't want to rush things anyway. Sweetly in the bone marrow he felt something he hadn't felt in years. Not love, of course, which only made the bones heavy, the blood thick and creamy, the head strong, adult, forceful; but romance—lightness, fret, phone calls: and all this in the dead of winter.

"May I see you again, or do you just do museums?"

"No, I have other settings. I'd like to see you again."

"A roommate answers the phone? Some petulant hanger-on? Half dachshund, perhaps?"

"Nobody but me."

58

"By the way, do you have a name or anything?"

"Eve Sample. I find it helps." First act, Mayfair, comedy. Smartchat.

"I'm Max Jamison." Super-critic. He laid out his wares casually. A few small gems, but flawless.

"And what do you do for a living?"

"I'm a writer."

She smiled, "Oh, *that* Max Jamison." Perfect. The fire bell clanged dolorously. Max was off and running.

Max was happy to walk home by himself. For how long now, he had felt that sadness was the last word. That he owed it to Justin to be sad. That if he wasn't sad, he could only be empty; there were no other choices.

And now, breaking through his timetable of gloom, the light sadness of morning and the heavy stone on his chest at night, and the quills of irony digging into his brow all day, came this goofy release. The chance to think about a girl's face. Wide-apart blue eyes, fair, wide forehead, gold lashes—just to think about things like that again; not to go to bed with them, not for a long time if ever, but just to have a nice thought at three in the morning instead of the gaseous horrors.

He walked home slowly, exulting. In three months or so, he would hold her hand. Then a kiss on top of the head, there, there, Magnolia. Let imagination go no further for now. Dancing together, walking, laughing. Most pathetic ruse of all—to be a boy again.

part two

8

"I'm rather disappointed in Max Jamison," said Professor Godfrey, massaging the chalk into his coat. "I would never have guessed he would come to this."

"Are you sure he was really so promising?" insinuated Sam Plinth, his bearded assistant. "I don't remember him when he was here, of course, but nothing he's done since I've been reading him has impressed me much."

"I *think* he was promising," said Godfrey, his wits wandering engagingly. "So many of them are, of course."

"That's it," said Plinth. "That's *it*. Promises, promises. I have three Max Jamisons in my class right this minute, promising the moon."

"What goes wrong?" wailed Godfrey. "What happens to the young rascals?"

"I will spare you the usual list of pitfalls," said Plinth —who was himself promising, and so must still tread carefully. "In Jamison's case, it seems to have been a routine failure to grow. After two years, the *aperçus* of youth were all gone, spent like 1925 Deutschmarks. High time for the brokerage business, you'd say. Time to do a Rimbaud, if you prefer. Retire before they discover the sore arm. But our lad is too deep in the web by then. Moist-eared poetasters are acclaiming him the cat's meow. 'The best of our younger critics.' So dig on he must."

"You depress me terribly," whined Godfrey. And added, almost in a whisper, "In so many ways."

"Jamison has this rigid quality, sometimes known as integrity, sometimes known simply as 'this rigid quality.' Upholding standards like a minor customs official, while genius slips quietly by. Vulgar, sleazy old genius, that knows no standards."

"You go too far," averred Godfrey.

"Worse, Jamison believes that wit has of itself some critical value. He believes that something said amusingly has more force than something said plainly. He believes . . ."

Godfrey groaned. "And now you say he's gone to *Now* magazine? Whatever that is."

"Yes, he's handed in his little tin star. Even the integrity, the petty bureaucrat's authority, is gone. Leaving only wit, swollen by now like a comedian's sausage . . ."

"Plinth!" Godfrey screamed, and made a wild lunge

across the desk. "You will not speak like that about Max. A good boy, gone to seed, if you like, if you must. But better on his worst day than some turgid little fart like yourself . . ."

Max sent white knight spinning into queen for a clipping penalty. Doing chess puzzles had once seemed passably restful but now it tossed him violently among imaginary dialogues, all of which he lost. He had forced the issue here, by giving Godfrey a line out of context. But he knew that if he returned to the mesmerism of the puzzle, Plinth would take the attack again, and Max would be routed. (He was also depressed, as usual, by the badness of the dialogue as such: it suggested the kind of fiction he would write if he tried.)

His standing with the academic community did bother him slightly. That was where the muffled whispers originated. There were always new ones with thinner heads and thicker glasses than the last lot, lining the fence, waiting for you to gasp and stumble in the unbearable heat. Max had begun life as one of their own, a highbrow's darling, and he still had many old academic friends. But what about the best new ones?

End of Sunday. He had sobered up a little from Eve Sample, but he had her phone number and would use it. Expecting nothing special. She had let one thin, dusty beam into his old warehouse. Ugh, these metaphors. He used the number right away, as a matter of fact, although he knew she would still be out, just for the pleasure of phoning a girl again. Max, you're going nuts —her phone sounded delicious, with low, suggestive purrs and pregnant little silences, just the right length apart.

Enjoy it while you can. He was using the girl quite frankly as a tranquilizer or happy pill, to get him past his night thoughts. Borrowing her face, tucking it against his shield and staring at it steadily, as he rammed his way past Justin this once, and Charlie, and finally past Helen, and into a meadow of cowslips and barley and fluting Greek shepherds, where he slept like a goddamned angel.

The next morning, he rang her up first thing, and asked her if she wanted to go to the movies.

"It's seven o'clock," she said. "Couldn't this have waited?"

"I was afraid you would go out somewhere. To an early class . . ."

"No one has classes this early. I feel as if I just got to bed. Couldn't you call back later?"

"I want to know if you'll go to the movies. Just say yes or no, and I'll let you go back to sleep."

"Thank you so much. What movies anyway? What are you talking about?"

"A screening, this afternoon. It's just a Western." He looked at the crumpled invite. "Called *Wagonwheels Westward.*"

"You woke me up just to tell me that?"

"Well, it's something to say. I guess I just wanted to hear how your voice sounded on the phone."

"So now you know."

"Yes, it's great."

"Really? At this time of morning?" The compliment roused her a pinch. "It sounds awful to me."

"A little furry maybe, that's all. A nice, sleepy voice."

"Yes, well, you see—that's the point."

66

"Don't hang up, Eve, please. Just say yes or no first."

"To *Wagonwheels Westward*? Can't you make me a better offer than that?"

"Well, how about *Three to Tango* at the Belasco, tomorrow night?"

"They don't still have plays with titles like that, do they?"

"I'm afraid so," he said.

"Look, I'm sleepy."

"Yes or no?"

"Ultimatums at this time of morning?"

"That's right."

"All right. No."

The conversation ruined his morning. He had agreed to review a creepy, malinformed history of the movies for *Now,* a fat, slatternly book with a wide, empty grin, and he couldn't concentrate on it worth a damn. He wanted to be playful and young with Eve, but at his age your feet hurt so quickly. He couldn't go the whole adolescent's route of cute invitations and arch rejections. At eleven he rang up angrily and said, "You awake yet?"

She said, "Yes. Why?"

"I want to get things straight. If you can only fit me in a week from next Wednesday, and if you can only make world premières of outstanding motion pictures, let's forget it."

"Forget what?"

"You know."

She was silent. Max was heavy-faced and frantic, after all. Answer this right, damn it, or hang up. I'm too old for games.

"You still insist on the *Wagonwheels?*" she said.

He saw the poverty of his gift and smiled despite himself. "It could be worse. I see some terrible things. You could share my pain. But I don't insist, as long as I see you somewhere, sometime."

"O.K., we'll make it *Wagonwheels.* Just this once."

They met at the screening room, and took the elevator in silence. She was subdued; even her skirt seemed longer than yesterday. This was his fault. He had put her in a silly position. She obviously didn't know what she thought about him yet. Out of who knows what senile fantasy or perhaps from seeing too many movies, he had imagined her in instant thrall to a fascinating older man. Clearly not so. He tried to make things light again, as they settled into their seats.

"I'm sorry, they don't sell popcorn here."

"Yes, I noticed."

"However, you can smoke."

"Thanks, I don't smoke."

They were interrupted by Kirk Douglas, chivying a group of settlers from East to West. Great toothy tantrums over nothing. Oh God, why did it have to be this? Three and a half hours of unrelieved nonsense. Her face was impassive. She didn't even find it funny.

He offered to leave at intermission, but she said, "You're supposed to stay, aren't you?" "*Rearview* doesn't care." "Why did you come at all? You knew what it would be like, didn't you?" "I thought I might do a piece on the New Westerns." "Then you'd better stay."

Again, they sat in the dark, and he wanted to embrace her, but saw this as an old man's wistful pass. He pictured the same old man following La Poupette home from the Follies, gimping along behind her with his champagne bottle and his bag of rare cheeses. Tonight's the night, mon vieux. No more sitting on deserted sidewalks, wringing one's hands. Bribe the concierge, storm the apartment, voilà!

This story was a better grade of trash than Kirk Douglas was offering. Of course, if he went on with it, La Poupette would finally laugh at him and empty his champagne over his head. Silly old man, you amuse me. Now take my number 3 garter and get lost. A fantasy followed its own laws, eventually.

Outside, indecisive, he said, "I'm sorry. I should never have forced you to see that."

"You didn't force me."

"Well, what?"

An impossible position for fair. What could she answer?

Mate in three moves. Asking a girl to see a lousy movie was an intolerable liberty. He hoped, at least, that she wouldn't pretend to have liked it. On the other hand, "I wanted to see you too" would not be quite right either.

"I didn't have a class today," she said. "So I thought, why not?"

"Do you have a class at dinnertime?"

She looked at him questioningly. They were still standing on the sidewalk, outside the screening building. Several colleagues were clustered around in the cold, burying the movie. Film critics were loungers and lingerers, he decided. They never had anywhere to go. It was always four o'clock in the afternoon, a bad time.

And they lived in small apartments off air shafts, sur-
rounded by huge gloomy posters. Well?

"I'm not dressed for dinner," she said. "I wasn't expecting it."

"I know I'm not handling this very deftly. Will you
come, though?"

"Why don't we make it another night? You can invite
me properly."

"No."

"What do you mean, 'no'?"

"I mean 'no.' If you're free for dinner, let's eat. If
you've got a class, let's not eat. I'm just too old to crap
around with dating diplomacy."

He felt the dull dead-weight of his personality rolling
toward her, ready to crush her bones to powder. He
didn't want this: he wanted lightness and flirtation. But
this was what he usually got. He stood there, flexing his
bare hands in the icy wind. Thinking about his life with
women, the brutal lessons given and received, the style
he could never alter now. Max, you depress me. The
heavy body and mind bending them back and back.

"Well, I haven't got a class, and I haven't got an excuse, but it seems like a funny way to do things."

"I know. I'm sorry. Will you come?"

"I guess so. I don't know why."

They arranged for him to pick her up later. It was an
awkward arrangement, since she had to go one way and
he the other, but she would not invite him into her
apartment while she changed, and he certainly saw the
point of that. Anything that could be saved of distance
and detachment, he valued. She was quite solemn as
they parted; already he had reduced her to that. He

went back to his own apartment, vowing not to repeat himself. Not to depress her too quickly.

As he shaved, he thought as fast as he could about Eve. She could still turn into anything at this stage. Phony, desperate, the bad things first; or else, long shot of the year, the thing he needed. The suppleness not to give up on him. Some special Max Jamison grace. He slashed the soap off his face, tremendously excited. Tremendously determined. Not to screw up, not to do another Helen.

9

Several hours later, Max didn't know very much more, mainly through his own doing. He confirmed that she was very bright and receptive. Deferred to his judgment on food, because he knew the restaurant better than she. Dressed well again. Good English. Sound use of make-up. O.K.—now feed it into the computer and find your soul-mate.

Not only was this a repulsive approach to women, it didn't even work. He was being so careful about her mileage and insulation that he couldn't make out what kind of woman she was. He had lost his critical method with women.

What movies did she like? Didn't get to many movies. Her taste in those she saw sounded suspiciously like his own. Had she been peeking? How about plays? Not many plays. Nobody under eighty goes to plays any more. Politics? What politics?

"I guess there really is a gap, isn't there, between my age and yours? It's a boring thought, I lay no special claim to it . . ."

"I don't know. I thought the gap was a little lower down—between my age and the people younger."

"How old are you, if you don't mind my asking?"

"Twenty-seven."

Twenty-seven. Unmarried. Neurotic. Possibly hysterical. (Are you hysterical, dear?) Mature, bones formed —won't change on you. Grateful, undemanding. The computer would whir and whistle like a steam kettle, and disgorge a long streamer like a supermarket check: poise, grooming, bone structure, $5.95.

"Generations now last two years and four months. So there are gaps all over. There were at least two between me and my wife."

"One and a half between me and my husband."

Married, divorced. Why? Demanding, fickle? husband a schmuck? Speak to me. Interpret the news. The computer's ghastly features lit in a grin. You can't even review plays like that, let alone women. Try to receive her, uncritically, like brand-new art. Judgment will follow.

"Husband?" he said.

"Yes. I'm afraid so."

"I'm sorry."

She shrugged. "It's over. Nothing to be sorry about."

"Children?"

"No."

73

Good. Trying to like somebody else's dwarf. Playing on the floor, with another man's leavings. The complexities of a new family, wrapping themselves round your legs. And yet—*why* no children? What kind of jaunty aridity was this? A brassy, self-sufficient girl, letting herself in at two in the morning, not noticing the emptiness of her smartass apartment, not caring. A selfish child.

Max, will nothing please you? What do you want from this girl, anyway? Two children, dead in a thunderstorm. Body unmarked by childbirth. Soul deep and tranquil. Thank God no one asked as much of him as he asked of women.

He saw himself as terrible company for a youngish girl. While you are sitting there deciding whether she is the perfect woman, she is collecting her things and leaving. Forgive me—I just want to be sure; I couldn't stand another mistake. Well, that's too bad, honey. We all have to take our chances. I can find my own way out.

Wait one minute. Can I take you home to meet my son? A child's eye view might help. Max remembered the kind of women he himself had liked as a boy. Cool, trustworthy, precise in their tenderness. Not his own mother, for Godsake, who was none of those things. Aunt Amy, the book reader, was getting warmer. Betsy Fothergill, playing a shrewd back court in her bloomers. A few others. Ingrid Bergman. Ethel Barrymore. Not Mary Martin.

Eve must be getting restless. He should be entertaining her in some way. So he began, like a medieval clown with one trick for All Saints' Day, to tell her about last week's plays. One or two phrases from his reviews that

74

he thought rather good, a joke he'd used on Saturday night. She began instantly to brighten. She laughed at the damn joke, giving him a sweet pain in the lumbar region. No, stop it, don't laugh, don't take advantage. She smiled warmly at his retreaded cleverness, right into his eyes. She was admiring him, by God. And he had trusted her! She was conning him, soothing him with admiration. And, sick at heart, he was loving it.

He would not, at any rate, sleep with her tonight. Not have another student opening up for him. Get to know each other first, develop a mature relationship. Yet even as he decided this, the desire was churning up steadily, his hand was reaching toward hers with melancholy certainty. The student had decided, and it was really up to the student. Max was basically an elective.

Then, later, the mature relationship.

Your father is a vain, silly man. So full of moral seriousness, so uncompromising. You should see his reviews. Wisdom, oh my God yes. Gravity. The Works. Then watch him creeping through the Sunday paper looking for little tads of praise. Big wise man scavenging in garbage cans. Or flirting with strangers, sucking praise from them, squeezing it out of them.

Helen II, the name he gave his conscience, started up as he paid the check and did not leave off until he was under the covers and too busy to listen. The compulsion to philander had dogged him through both marriages, especially after bouts of hard work. It was always brief, one night or two, by which time he could see his mistake perfectly well. He would meet the girl at a party and flirt like a maniac until he got her to bed. Then, right there, in the middle of things, he would start to sober up. The girl was like a seal of approval for work completed, a kiss from a French general. The pay was so rotten you needed something.

Unfortunately, Max was no liar, he felt lying would harm his work, so he had to defend himself as best he could when his wives inevitably found out. E.g.: "I have to get love from somewhere, Helen, and I don't get much from you any more."

"You might try giving some."

"I do. It's a silly thing to have to say."

"Oh, Max—you just don't know, do you? That isn't love you give me, it's sentimentality. Sex makes you feel good, and you magnanimously decide to give some of the good feeling back. This you call tenderness."

"You could make a bum out of any emotion with that kind of reasoning."

"No—just yours."

"What else is anybody's tenderness? If you break it down like that."

"I can't tell you. You can't break other people's tenderness down like that."

"Ah—mystical hogwash. 'I can't tell you'" he mimicked, blindly, "'you wouldn't understand.'"

"Well?"

This was a lunchtime discussion. He had come back from a night out, tired and spiritually disarranged, and she was dressed for housework, her hair in a bun, protecting the decencies against this slug.

"What was her name this time?"

"Cynthia."

"Clever of you to remember."

"I make a big effort. Look—I don't see what you've

got to complain about. You don't give a hell of a lot of love yourself, so we're even on that score. Maybe neither of us knows how. So, you don't want me yourself—why do you mind if somebody else gets a piece?"

She began to stack the dishes. The children's and hers. His dirty ones were elsewhere. "I don't mind that as such. I mind about the trivial damage you do. Strutting around, using these poor girls to bolster your self-esteem, so you won't have to face yourself and change. You haven't grown at all—excuse me, I know you hate the word . . ."

"That's all right. As a matter of fact, I face myself a sickening amount of time."

"You're trapped. You have new ideas but they're all the same, the same *kind* of ideas. You write the same kind of sentences . . ."

"Leave my sentences out of this," flashed Groucho Jamison.

"Everything is so hopeless. You've built this structure and you can't get out of it. But so long as you find some girl, some *new* girl, to tell you it's all right, you don't have to face it."

"So what do I do instead? LSD? Blow my mind, swing a little?"

"LSD would blow you apart. One crack in your beautiful façade, your great version of yourself, and you'd be gone."

The critic in him saluted. This was the truth. But wasn't it also the truth about anyone who amounted to anything? You built a personality, a style, and you were trapped by it. Otherwise you were a slack-faced nobody.

He hated her damn healthiness, her dumb openness to life. Did *she* have any great ideas? You bet your sweet fanny she didn't. She just spewed this second-hand garbage, which was once the property of minds like his own, minds made of stiff hard plaster. You couldn't have ideas independent of style. You needed a personality to operate.

"You *might* try psychoanalysis. The structure could be dismantled, stone by stone."

"Jewish finishing school. Look, I don't want my structure dismantled. I'd be just like everybody else. I'd write like everybody else, and think like everybody else. You may not believe this, but I value what I've learned to do. I think I'm a pretty good critic."

He was tired, he wouldn't normally say that. She shrugged. "You've come to the end of the line, Max, that's all. Good line, bad line, what difference does it make now? You just can't go any further in that direction. You'll be writing the same pieces thirty years from now."

He shuddered; there was a ghastly possibility here. What a terrible trick, to play on a writer's uncertainty. How many nights had he woken, half strangled, knowing it was all over. His arm had gone to sleep, those golden fingers would type no more. The night was filled with old phrases and formulas, bat wings, insects made of black fur. The basic Max Jamison sentence clogged his eardrums. He would never improve on it now. For years, he had been building a cenotaph and calling it a career.

"Writing is a skill," he explained carefully, to himself

and Helen. "If I get stuck, I must find the answer within the limits of that. You don't tell a tennis player to improve his character, you tell him to improve his game."

"Yes, professor. I remember."

"Besides, my character is not as static as you think. You only have the one approach to it, so it always seems the same to you. But it changes, it takes in new material . . ."

"I'm happy to hear it."

"O.K., forget it. I'm sorry I brought it up." These conversations left him broken and exhausted. If she was right, as she well might be, there was nothing he could do about it. Her serenity drove him crazy. Are *you* growing, sweetie? Do you have any problems in that line? Helen, too, would have the same ideas thirty years hence, but they would be perennially healthy and life-enhancing.

Unfortunately, he respected her intelligence, if not the rut of jargon in which it operated. He should never have allowed her to stop being a student. When did she escape? Ah, they all escaped eventually. Eve here would escape. That's what he had against students, why he didn't want any part of them. They wound up breaking your heart.

There was nothing like making love to another girl to remind him of Helen. His arbiter of taste. He stroked Eve's breast lazily, flipping the nipple with his fingers, waiting for the mistake to become apparent. Helen had helped him to see them all as mistakes; people who would have to be defended with a red face over breakfast. More stones for his cenotaph. But after a few minutes he realized that no defense was needed this time. The moves had all been good, even the taxi and elevator conversation had been right, in spite of Helen II's nagging. He had somehow convinced himself that this was serious, that he wasn't putting in for a cheap reward. Something like affection fluttered in his mind—a reaching out to the other person. He wasn't just swaggering and showing off: he loved this girl, a little bit.

Or was that just one of her tricks?

They had breakfast together in dreamy silence. She made no declarations, no appeals. He was getting eyestrain, looking for clues in her behavior. Max was a man who liked his breakfast. He had slept better than he had in months, and it was nice to have someone else cook his eggs. He snorted over the drama review, and again over the movie review. Eve came over and brushed against him, to see what the snorting was about. He explained that it was just a habit.

"I have a morning screening. Do you want to come?"

"Any special movie?" She smiled.

"Never mind. Just say yes or no." They had a joke.

He liked her apartment fine. The paintings were right for a single girl in a sunny room. He wondered if someone else had chosen them for her. It was too early to get jealous, but not too early to gather material for jealousy.

"You know," he said, "my ideas about romance, courtship, whatever you call this stuff—"

"You don't call it anything just yet."

"Right. Anyhow, those ideas have changed quite a bit since I started going to movies as well as plays."

"How is that?"

"Well," he grinned, "it's quicker in movies, for one thing. All those naked shoulder blades. One minute they're snooping around Berlin, complete strangers, and the next they're lying thoughtfully side by side, swapping trade talk."

"You think we're a movie scene?"

"Well, I didn't bring flowers to the stage door for six months, I didn't ask you to the prom."

"Is that bad?"

"I don't know, I guess not."

Suddenly, there was a barrier. Why had he put it up? Because he did not believe in going as fast as they had. He had to establish that. In actual fact, he went as fast as anyone, but he didn't believe in it—that was what being old-fashioned stood for. Not believing in what you were doing.

She moved away, and he thought, I've raised issues she doesn't want to hear, cracked the glass bell in which she lives. Dundering fairy godfather, dropping a black hairy toad in the magic soup. But she wasn't angry.

"We'll go slower in the future," she said, smiling. "I wasn't being modern, if that's what you think. I just thought we'd reached that point . . ."

"Oh yes, we had." He felt like wringing his hands. He didn't want to go slower in the future, not the least bit; just wanted to establish what he felt about these things in general. Then on with the dance.

"Let's get dressed," she said. And, of course, stay dressed. She was wearing a transparent pink nightgown, and he hadn't the faintest desire to get dressed. But he had talked himself into it. Glumly he complied.

Proving oneself a mature, responsible adult had its penalties.

Once dressed, they tried a little more conversation. Getting to know each other the old way. Mother and father and background. Some other time, baby. The movie way was infinitely better. Yet, as they talked, he began to enjoy himself. Just talking to a pretty woman was nice, once you had adjusted your hopes downward. He began telling her about Justin and his astounding sensibility. She listened as women are supposed to, with bright sympathy. For a minute, he felt he had found a dignified moral solution—to be talking about his son to the Other Woman. He was doing his duty by Justin, was satisfying his own requirements, was being a serious man.

"What about your other child? You said you had two."

"Oh yes, Charlie. He's a good boy, too. Very self-reliant. I think he likes his mother better than me, but then they're supposed to at that age."

"You can't tell. Maybe Charlie is the one who really needs you."

Don't tell me how to run my shop. Bright sympathy was one thing, but no know-it-all maternal wisdom, please. "You may be right," he said politely.

"Shall we go? I do have a class this time." Of course, she couldn't make the screening. The old courting schedule demanded an interval. He wanted to pull out all his screening invitations and theater tickets and say, Can you make Tuesday, can you make Wednesday. But he must select now a really worthwhile opening, and she must deliberate before accepting. Send her answer on the butler's tray.

They agreed to make it four days hence, at the new Ingmar Bergman movie. She loved Bergman and was dying to see it. Next, if bad breath didn't interfere, the Senior Prom itself.

10

Up, up and away. Lecture dates were the pea in the shoe of his profession. Flying would have been all right, if he could just stop hearing "You Are My Sunshine" in the jet engines; a massed choir. By a violent effort, he was able to switch it to "My Old Kentucky Home." The plane did not play accidentals, so he could only get the choir to do simple tunes.

He had a letter about that in his pocket right now. "It is manifest that you really like musicals, and are too snobbish to admit it." You must be kidding, Jasper. He had been getting that letter every year since he began. Almost as often as, "Mr. Jamison, why are you so full of hate? I'm really sorry for you, you know that, you pig?"

Here was a more serious one. "The notion that anyone can write about movies is, I realize, a prevalent one these days. However, I never expected to see it in currency at *Rearview*. Max Jamison is, I suppose, adequately equipped to criticize the theater, but he knows nothing whatever of movies and has no sense of the medium. He is both condescending and insecure. When he talks about camera technique, he sounds like a child reciting the Gettysburg Address."

The sun shines bright on my old Kentucky home, please don't take my sunshine away. If he mixed the two, it would take a little longer to go insane. Valuable time gained.

Ah, these movie buffs. He had honestly had no idea how grim and implacable they were. Luckily, they were usually also inarticulate. He would demolish a couple of them during the question period this afternoon. Still, they kept coming. They held life cheap, flung themselves on you like moths, strange venomous little people with a secret, a cause.

A jet flew overhead and away, and he watched it straining upward like a shark cleaving the Caribbean. Electronics had their moments. Make a note to stop being snotty. His martini made him briefly mellow. There was something gorgeous going on up here. Max was with it for a moment.

He wrote a few lines in his head. Something about a blurred filter. The hell I don't know movie technique. Buffs have to say things like that. They can't abide trespassers. Also, they distrust literacy. Their idea of a movie genius is an incoherent baboon who points and says "I want that." Buffs. True cinema. True cinema values. Ah, so. *I spent several days in Paris with Pierre*

85

Pantoufle, the great director, as he shot his new film, Kiss Me Baby, *a black satire on American power, and I was astounded by the purity of his feeling about film. He always insists on ten minutes of* absolute *silence at the beginning. Nobody moves or breathes. And then, a tinny clatter of scissors, falling from the girl's hand. She has cut her wrists, you see.*

Quite. Max was getting sleepy. He shut his eyes, and saw the black malignant blood snaking over the girl's hand. Her eyes stare. Suddenly the screen cracks like a mirror. Pure cinema. Quite.

He was met at the airport by a group of students. Academic world now. Dean's office, Harkness Building, room thirty-five thousand and six, walk two miles down the corridor and bear left at the forty-eighth water cooler—Max blankly followed the trail to the inevitable man with the rimless glasses and the pale pink handshake.

Our students are very interested in film, are they, the buggers? Yes, they even make their own, roll them behind the gym, expect you'll find them a lively group, look forward challenging last week we had—Max knew deans from way back, and dean talk. Also heads of departments, with their encouraging enrollments, and assistant bursars, with their nagging requests for your Social Security number. And then the long, graceless ritual. Academics did everything so badly, entertained badly, poured sherry badly.

Once on the platform, he was safe. Of course, he was introduced badly, given credit for someone else's book and placed on the wrong magazine. But after that, he was free to do things his own way—namely, well. He

86

felt the old weary arrogance returning. He liked teaching—introducing children to the ways of thought, taking their watery minds and plunging a hot divining rod into them. How would they know, with their English II's and their dean's offices, that ideas are personal, idiosyncratic, or they are not ideas at all.

"Mr. Jamison, I get a feeling from your criticism that you are *too* much concerned with ideas." His first buff. Explain yourself, young man.

"I don't know. It just seems to me that there's more to movies than just ideas."

"Well, why don't you work that out a little bit, and perhaps we can talk about it next time. Next question."

"I didn't think you were fair to the last questioner."

"You didn't? That's funny. I thought I was. All right, I'll try again. *Of course there is more to movies than just ideas.* Is that better? Part of an education is to learn to recognize a, shall we say, unrewarding question and not to waste too much time on it."

"Yes sir."

"Any other questions?"

"Yes sir. I am not quite sure what you mean by ideas. I know that you're in favor of them in a general way, but when I read your criticism I don't find too many. You seem to treat films and plays quite unintellectually —in fact, you crack a few jokes, poke fun at the plot, pat the actors on the head, praise the direction, whatever that means . . ."

Max's hand shook and jammed his cigarette against his lip. Not because of the question, but because of the questioner, a gorgeous blonde whose hips swayed with lilting earnestness while she talked. A pupil, a natural pupil. Oh God, this was ridiculous.

That question is best answered in bed, he wanted to say. Instead, he gave some dreary forgettable retort about how few works deserved intellectual discussion, and the mistake of reviewing things beyond their merits.

"But you make jokes about Jean-Luc Godard."

"Exactly."

He hoped he wouldn't meet her afterwards. He couldn't face the look, the candid eyes; he would have to take her and fill her with his personality and mind, cram her quickly, as for some crazy exam, and creep back to New York empty and shrunken.

He had agreed to go to the dean's reception—well, he was the one who was being received, so he had better go. If there was one thing academics did more badly than anything else in the world, it was receiving people. Standing around in thin-faced embarrassment, too shy to speak or even to look at you. Whispering to their colleagues in remote corners of the room. Then lunging at you suddenly with a prize student. "Sorry, the ice hasn't come. We forgot to order Scotch, is this all right, it says, er, blended whiskey."

They trooped into the dean's study for the grim charade, and of course she was there, somebody's prize student, eyes shining, greedy for Jamison. He tried to keep his distance, with the help of swift incantations. "You have just met Eve. You are embarked on something serious. You do not need another student. Your classload is full." Circle along the wall, brushing the books for luck with his shoulders, plunging into conversation with the

Athletic Director, out again, a few words about the new library with some fat fool—and all the time her eyes, burning for education, raking him like a searchlight.

A few hours later in a sickening, coy motel, designed expressly for this, to cater to his insanity, he sat on the bed with his mission discharged, trying to find something to say. She wanted to be an actress. He told her she would probably make a good one. He believed it. Oh yes, he did. Read lines well. Perhaps he could tell her some people to see. That would be awfully kind. She would certainly look him up in New York. That would be awfully nice.

Your father is a— Shut up, Helen! Imagine not spotting an acting major, laying up nuts for the long winter, thinking that a critic could help her, any critic. He pictured the life ahead of her, all the floors she would sit on, the blank faces of helpful men, and thought, why doesn't she kill herself now. Pure cinema. He next tried to think of her as a nice, intelligent kid, which, for all he knew, she was, but he found that he didn't care one way or the other. He didn't want to teach her anything today. He had nothing to teach anyway. He was a posturing windbag, with the wind all gone for now.

He put on his trousers, and swore to cut down his lecturing.

11

Justin looked as if he knew just what Daddy had been up to this week. So did the cat. Max was feeling a little jumpy today. Helen wanted to talk to him about money. She handed him a stack of bills too big for his pockets: Justin's piano lessons, Justin's teeth, Justin's flu shots. It made Max want to force his way back into their lives immediately. He wanted to be around when Justin's teeth fell out and when he reeled from his flu shot.

It wasn't much fun for anybody if he spent the afternoon feeling sentimental. So he made a prodigious effort to be amusing. It wasn't his thing, Max was not a funny man in that sense, but Justin gave a startled laugh anyway: must be frightening for him, big man, big face, trying to be funny.

Are you happy to see me, Justin? What has Mummy been saying? Justin was looking out the bus window again, this boy was really hooked on bus windows. Max looked forward to this meeting all week, but he fumbled with it when the time came.

"How's school?"

"All right."

"I haven't seen a report card lately."

"I didn't get one lately."

"Oh."

Am I still influencing your development? Are my ideas getting through to you somehow or other? Will you grow to look less like me as you go along—no longer conforming your facial expressions to mine, but giving your mother custody of the face? Would you be happy without me? Would it perhaps be unselfish and admirable if I stopped seeing you altogether? I should like to do something unselfish and admirable. It would teach your mother a lesson. But I can't let you go.

There were many interesting things to talk about, but he couldn't talk about any of them. Did Justin know why Daddy had left home, for instance? And did Justin worry about it? They sat together in diplomatic silence. Max didn't know whether you traumatized kids by bringing up those things. It seemed likely. He was getting bored with being with Justin, because he wasn't allowed to talk to him about anything.

"Will you buy me a Whiz-bangeroo, Daddy?"

"What's that?"

"It's a thing they have on television. It's neat."

"I don't trust things they have on television."

"Will you get it for me? Please."

"I guess so."

"And will you get me a midget rocket launcher?"

"We'll see."

"I'll give you a list of things I want, O.K.?"

Who was this scheming gnome? Max looked with horror into the bubbling eyes. When they got to the movies, Justin would yammer for candy and popcorn and Pepsi-Cola. Daddy was the man who bought you things. There was some point to Daddy after all.

"Do you ever wonder why I left home?" Better a little trauma than to turn the boy into a sleek capon, a wheezing gobbler.

"Mommy told me."

"What did she tell you?"

He shrugged. "*You* know. That you didn't get along." He seemed bored with the question. According to Helen, he had shown no interest, had barely seemed to be listening, when she first brought it up. But for several nights afterward he had cried in his sleep; his first encounter with bad dreams.

"Do you miss me?"

"Oh, sure."

"Well, I'm still your father, you know. I'll always be that."

"Yeah, I know."

Well—so much for that. Justin returned to contemplating gifts that he wanted. He slept soundly these nights, lulled by thoughts of profit and capital gains.

Daddy had deserted him, to be sure—what a reason to leave, that *they* didn't get along. Really!—but he was still good for a touch. And gifts, hardware, property, were more dependable things than so-called love, anyway. The boy slept in a magic bower of greed.

. . . Helen, can't you do something about this? He realized that every crotchet that Justin developed from here on in would seem like a direct consequence of his own leaving. He wanted quickly to plead his case with Justin—it wasn't just my idea, leaving; your mother thought it was a marvelous idea. She said all of you were trapped in the cave of my mind—she's some fancy prose stylist, your mother. She compared me to a big black crow or swamp buzzard. She said that I brought death with me, in my beak. Lots of pretty things like that.

So you can see why I left, perhaps. Or can't you? It's bad to be told that you carry death with you. Believe me.

By the end of the afternoon, a gaseous Disney afternoon, with Justin chomping remorselessly at his side, he had worked up one of the old-time rages at Helen. He would smash in the door and fetch her a crack on the snout. My God, the things she had called him—after which he would demand she take him back, for the sake of the children.

When he got to the apartment with Justin, he found Helen in a rather peculiar mood too. She made a crack about the amount of candy Justin had manifestly been eating. He did look woebegone, with brown cheeks and brown teeth and a great sodden listlessness about him. But usually Helen let that pass. Any little sign of humanity in Max should be encouraged, even at the cost of a belly ache.

"We must have a talk," she said, but when they sat down in the study, she didn't seem to have anything specific to say. She murmured something about money again, "now that you're making so much," but money wasn't one of her things. She asked if he had any fresh plans, a new girl. He said no plans, no girl. He really didn't know whether he had a girl or not. Besides, this was classified information insofar as she was concerned.

"What about you, Helen? Anything happening?" She shrugged. She must have her own secrets, or at least pretend to. So as to come to the conference table as equals.

"What about the divorce?" he said. "Do you want to start work on that?"

"I don't know."

"What is it we must talk about then?"

"I don't know."

She was looking or listening for something, an electric signal, from him. To see if what she called death, the heavy look in the eyes, the gravedigger's spade of a tongue, had left him. Yes, honey, I've reformed. I've gutted my last play. I'm opening that little bookstore, that adorable little writer's workshop. From now on I'm going to build things, not tear them down.

She must have seen by now that the big jolly man hadn't changed. No positive blips today. She uncrossed her legs and braced them like a goalie. Her thighs,

under tight brown slacks, had a strange, isolated interest for Max, all that was left.

"We don't quarrel so much, that's one nice thing," he
said.

"That's true. I'm sorry about all that. What was the
use anyway?"

"It seemed worthwhile at the time."

"Yes, I suppose so."

"Are you lonely, Helen?" She seemed to be talking for
the sake of talking.

"No lonelier than before."

"You mean when you were living with old icy-fingers:
Max Jamison, boy-embalmer?"

"The same."

"I see. Well, it's good we don't quarrel any more."

"I'm sorry, I see we could start again without too
much trouble." She was picking brocade off the chair,
which annoyed him. If this were his house, he would be
forced to speak to her. Irritation was built into the fin-
gernails of their relationship.

"Look, Max. I'll tell you what it is. I'm not judging
you any more, or hoping things for you either. To you,
you're all right, which is more than most people can say.
We'll settle for that. But"—she paused, and there was a
rending of brocade that almost made him scream—"I
want to go away, all the way away, from you. Take the
boys and go."

"Where? Why?"

"Why is easy. Because we still live under your
shadow here. And your shadow weighs. *You* can carry
it. Little boys can't. Justin is nervous all day after he

sees you. He thinks he looks forward to seeing you, but you should see how awful he looks at the end of the afternoon. I don't know what you talk about, it doesn't matter."

"Oh, come on. What we talk about is school and the toys he wants. Doesn't everybody?"

"It's a great shadow that comes and goes, and it's too heavy for him."

"I knew I shouldn't have taken you to all those lousy plays. 'Shadows, Lord Ravenal—they're the undoing of us all.' "

"Funny?"

"I don't know. I just think you're talking a lot of crap, that's all. But don't let me disturb you."

"All right, I won't. Then there's Charlie. This is quite beyond me. You treat Charlie as if he were some kind of small, malignant insect . . ."

"You're crazy."

"It's true, it's true, you treat him like some little thing you have to hold at the end of the tongs."

"Stuff it, Helen. I play with Charlie every Saturday, and you know it. Right down on the damn floor."

"Yes, and such playing. Such giddy romps. You look as if he's going to bite your finger and poison it. However, I didn't mean to analyze your play techniques. It's just your attitude."

"You'd be a happy, fruitful woman if you'd never heard that word, attitude."

"You don't like Charlie, and you're too self-ignorant to hide it."

"Self-ignorant," he repeated thoughtfully.

96

"Charlie knows it, and he's wretched about it. He's still in diapers you know, he doesn't want to grow up."

"Because of Batwing Griswold, your weekly visitor from the Valley of the Fallen."

"Justin you do like, in your own way. You identify with him or something."

"Christ, I'd like to win one round around here."

"But you're making him just as wretched as Charlie anyhow. Your love and your hatred come to the same thing."

"Did I tell you you were crazy?"

"Yes."

"What manner of facile bullshit is this? Hatred is akin to love. The truest comedy is close to tragedy. Hug me, Amelia, and then walk away quickly. All that mindless pishposh. You really want to have that brain looked at by a good play doctor."

"Have you anything to say about the *subject*?"

"You haven't learned a thing, I taught you nothing. Oh well. You can't win them all. The subject? Oh yes, that. Well, you can't take the kids away without my permission, and of course I'm not giving it."

"We'll see."

Which more or less ended the conference. Max tried to say a more ample goodbye than usual to Charlie on the way out, but it seemed like a sham. Charlie's eyes were large and bored. He didn't have Justin's economic interest in this strange man, and could barely remember him from week to week. Must do more about Charlie. Justin was in the bathroom, as well he might be. They said goodbye through the door. It occurred to

Max, as a bleak consolation on the way home, that although to be sure a thousand maggots were eating away his brain and liver, and the bamboo shoots under his toenails were pressing a bit, he was probably no more beset by trouble than the next man. He was just about in the American mainstream.

12

Winter is the time of year when they say, "We have assembled a distinguished panel to discuss this ever-green question. On my left is, on my right is, author of several books names of which escape me, distinguished, merciless wit, has been called the most in America since Percy Hammond. Corrosive style. Biting wit, biting merciless wit. Let's start with Mr. Jamison."

Max coughed. He could recite his thing about "the role of the critic," backward and in Swahili by this time. He writhed when chairmen went on about his wit. "You fools, you blundering fools," he wanted to cry. But panels were like jury duty, a critic logged his so many hours a lifetime, like a good citizen.

"My wit doesn't really bite. If it did, Doctor Wandsworth wouldn't be so cheerful about it. Nor are my thoughts on tonight's subject especially corrosive. I believe, first of all . . ."

The thread gets thinner as you continue winding. Believe in the role of the critic. Who really gives a shit? All you night-school students, hear me out. For many thousands of years, including several Golden Ages, a few Silvers, at least one Bronze, and some less distinguished material, civilization got on swimmingly without critics. Sophocles hacked along somehow without them (or did he? well, I'm sure he could have). Shakespeare, and all that. Then some meddling ass invented critics. Why? For night students, of course. With their shining eyes and their glowing tails.

"Thank you, Mr. Jamison. A most eloquent defense of criticism, I must say. What do you think, Mr. Glass?"

"I agree with Max, on the whole, and would just like to add . . ."

Glass was an impossibility, a critic who liked to be liked. He wanted to please Max, and also the other panelists who hadn't yet spoken. This made him a mite tentative. At the other end of the panel glowered Harold Bruffin, well-known angry man, who couldn't stand to be liked by anyone. The fourth member, Frank Spangle, was a lapsed Englishman—languid and whimsical and nothing to fear. "It occurred to me while you chaps were talking that, had there been critics in the agora, Aeschylus would never have given the *Agamemnon* such a potty ending," etc. You didn't bother to please such a man, you just gave him some old trouser buttons to play with.

Bruffin was something else, though. He would chew

you up, even if you had just repeated one of his own articles word for word. Rage was his fuel, his motive, his whole aesthetic. His face was angry in repose, with just that touch of playfulness that can make a critic really brutal. He would frisk with Glass, maul him a little, send him home broken and torn.

Glass got to the end of his statement, which God knows was inoffensive enough and Bruffin swiveled into position. He tested his microphone with a roar. "Yes, well. To begin with, I believe that one thing the critic can*not* do is what Mr. Jamison attempts to do—that is, to cut himself in half, and review two ways for two magazines. Jamison is, or was, quite a good critic. Limited but firm. Very good in his detail work. But now that he is servicing the simple readers of *Now*, he has given all that up and become, as one must, a mere gag-man."

Max had gathered by now that he and not Glass was on the menu tonight. He experienced the brief thrill, like the onset of fever, of having his paranoia come true. So *that's* what they thought of him out there.

"I don't blame Max. I would probably have taken the job myself. I merely mourn the loss of a critic. And mourn a system that causes this to happen."

The chairman was sincerely flustered. People hired Bruffin to behave like this, but then they got scared when he did. Max supposed he must play with Bruffin. He was exhilarated for now, but later he would ache all over. "Harold is too kind. He is, you know, not altogether a bad critic himself. His inlay work is particularly fine, though he falls down occasionally on his root canals. Of course, I considered the things he has brought up tonight, before I took the job at *Now*. Purity is a big word with our set. Writing impeccable reviews, year after year, for impeccable readers. Or, on the other hand, bringing the theater to a larger group, the American public . . ."

"You don't think you're doing that, do you, Max?" Bruffin snarled. "I see the same crowd at the theater I always saw, before you began to bring the American public in. They still have to keep the heat turned up for the Scarsdale matrons."

"Maybe, maybe. I admit, there isn't a hell of a lot you can do for the New York theater, at those prices and with those habits. But there is a whole nation to consider here. Don't you think it important that a national magazine like *Now* bothers to run a theater column at all? And don't you think it valuable that they hire a man from one of the little magazines?"

Bruffin sighed, which sounded like a high wind through that microphone. "Max, I don't know why I bother to argue with you. You know the answer to all that stuff better than I do. I don't blame you for trying to kid yourself about it, but for the sake of the audience, let me refresh your memory for a moment. Yes, it would be nice, yes it would be valuable—if you could review the way you used to. Without the jokes, without the simplifications. Talking about jokes—you made better ones in the old days by accident than you do now when you're trying."

"You have to make some concessions."

"Some concessions. Whew. WHEW." (Bruffin raked the mike again.) "Yes, you could say that, I guess. Space limitations this week, chop-chop. Out goes your best paragraph. Max, you're coming in too long. Couldn't you get to the point a little quicker. Who is this guy Marat/Sade anyway? our readers want to know. Don't insult them, though. Just slip it in gently."

"You must have worked for one of those magazines yourself, Harold."

"I did, as a matter of fact. Years ago. As a book reviewer. I quit."

"Good for you. You might find that things have changed since then. The readers are assumed to be a little brighter. The writers, it is now understood, can afford to go elsewhere if they're unhappy."

"Max, Max. I know, I know. If you want to compare three versions of the *Three Sisters*, discuss Chekhov's development in terms of Tsarist politics, discuss the influence of French literature on Turgenev, you're perfectly free to do so. It's just that you don't choose to any more. Or to devote a whole column to one small performance. Or to analyze the sets or the lighting . . ."

"You're a snob, Harold. You don't even read *Now*, I can tell. I've been doing things like that ever since I got there."

"Yes—Turgenev, the well-known nineteenth-century Russian novelist and playwright, went to Paris, the well-regarded capital of France, in the year—"

"Gentlemen, gentlemen. This is very interesting, but I think it's time we heard from our other panelists. What do you think, Mr. Spangle?"

"Well, I think a critic may be likened to a very small . . ." The fun was over. Max felt his soul for bruises and contusions. Harold's attack was familiar, of course—there was only one attack. The question was, did Bruffin speak for many, or was he winging it on his own? Takes a defrocked news-magazine man to point the finger at you, doesn't it? Bruffin sat there raging, burning up slowly, a curiously impersonal man.

Max could see Eve at the end of the five six seventh row, looking grave. Was her belief in him shaken? or was she rallying to his side like an earth-mother? His motive for being here at all was to impress her; but nobody looks impressive with his arms over his head. Warding off the blows of maddened little men.

Sell-out, cop-out, write-in, love-in, out, in. Everyone together now. He was restless and wanted to get off the platform. Spangle's smirk was driving him crazy. *How* could a critic be like a small stoat or chipmunk? What would be fun would be to empty a huge pan of water over Spangle's head. Then leap on the desk and announce the end of all panels, everywhere. After that, jump on Bruffin's back and go charging through the audience. Snortling like a dolphin.

"Max, what do you say to that?"

"Well, as a muddied hack, working for a news magazine, I'm not sure I should say anything. Without consulting Mr. Big and the stockholders."

"Come on, Max—don't be so touchy." Glass, pinned to the wall with an assagai quivering in his crotch. Up the revolution!

"I think the whole thing is a glorious waste of time. Meeting of minds, you say? There are no more than two or three minds in any generation, and they arrange never to meet. Very wisely. Criticism, needlework, field hockey, *in that order*, is what I say."

This time he had spoken, instead of merely thinking.

Certain barriers seemed to be breaking down. A man worried about his wife and child got irresponsible in other contexts, to make up.

Glass twittered. "Max, you're very violent tonight. Something you reviewed disagreed with you?"

"It's the nihilism of the sell-out," explained Bruffin. "If they can prove that *every*thing is a waste of time, then they're sitting pretty."

Bruffin, you want to settle this in the alley, or what?

"You see it all the time, with the talented men on news magazines. Violent cynicism. Self-loathing . . ."

"You're really talking about the talented men on the little magazines, aren't you?" said Max. "Men like Harold Bruffin—half insane from trying to be heard."

"My, my—this is a lively discussion," said the chairman; hoping, dismal twit, that saying this made everything all right.

"You're bright enough to make distinctions, Max. The cynicism of little magazines is a much better quality cynicism and you know it. Frustration over not reaching people is not so bad. Despair over reaching them with junk is something else."

"Cant, pure cant, Bruffin. Both despairs are the same. To the eye of a proctologist, your ass and mine are in exactly the same crack, Harold. Desperate about getting old and dying and not having changed anything—the theater, books, anything."

"Gentlemen, gentlemen! Gentlemen! What do you say, Mr. Spangle?" Lord save us, Mr. Spangle.

"I say it's marvelous to find such heat expended over such an ancient question."

You Americans are simply priceless. Max's desire to turn the thing into a physical shambles, an Arab street scene, was almost enough to act on by now. Critics hurtling in every direction, like flung salamis. Spangle trying to brake himself à la Harold Lloyd, plunging through plaster walls, and coming to rest like a moose head in the game room. Ah well, some other time perhaps.

When he got outside with Eve, he asked her quickly how he had done. "I know I should wait for you to tell me. But I seem to be in a hurry to know."

"You were fine."

"What does that mean?"

"Well, it means you kept your head when that awful man was attacking you."

"Did I win the argument, though?"

"I don't know. I'm a terrible judge of things like that. I'm sure you didn't lose it—if that makes any sense."

They were sitting at a long table with Glass and Spangle and assorted hangers-on. So they couldn't put together much of a conversation. Bruffin had refused altogether to come, as though going to bars was some kind of selling out. The chairman had gone off to count the house, after assuring everyone that it had been a lively meeting, much better than last week's.

"Where do you stand on selling out, anyway," whispered Max to Eve. "Are you for it?"

Eve blinked, under pressure of smoke. "I don't know that I understand it. I mean, I don't know why going to *Now* is a sell-out. That's why I don't know whether you won the argument."

"You're still young," said Max. "Harold and I are chil-

dren of the thirties. It must be like listening to two medieval theologians."

He touched Eve's hand, and found it cool. She had
been, he guessed, slightly bored by the whole thing. If
he had been with Helen, they would have been at the
screaming stage by now. "Harold was right. You were
saying the same things yourself five years ago. Remember when Hank Porter went to *Now?* 'Porter is a sell-
out, Porter is a sell-out . . .' "

Remember? Remember everything.

"Tell me about selling out. Is it fun?" Eve wanted in
on his thoughts. She had, he realized, an old-fashioned
quality after all—the flip style of the forties. He pictured her putting a cigarette in Bogart's mouth, between
the bandages.

"No, not especially," he said. "You have to have the
right wife for it. Most wives are right enough, I guess. A
lot of them insist on it, in fact. I was just unlucky."

Max had indeed been shocked by the vehemence of
Helen's reaction to his humble sell-out. Why did a
woman who had already given up on his criticism care?
Did she mind having a washing machine for the first
time? "Helen—is there anything I could do that would
please you? I've moved, I've changed."

"Yes, backwards."

"I'll have to write differently. More exposition, less
criticism. More patience."

"Yes, Max."

"What does that mean?"

"Yes, Max." Helen for once had smiled. Sell-outs explaining themselves were a riot. More patience indeed.
For the wee folk. He said, "All right, Helen. While

107

you're grinning is a good time to leave. I've had it. I'll, er, send for my stuff."

"All right."

"You sound surprised."

"Not especially. You've been looking like a man who's about to leave for some time. Waiting for a break in the conversation, so you can say goodbye properly. The minute you stopped being God, that was the end."

"I've hung in for quite a while since then." Down the ladder, God, cherub, seraph, fallen angel, pig.

"Yes, hoping to make a comeback, to be God again." Grunting around the pigsty, laying impossible plans for an uprising. The real God was a woman, probably an American housewife. Men don't qualify for God in any respect. They're built all wrong. "Now you know you can't. You've gone to *Now*. You've given up. You'll never be God again."

A woman shall crush your head. Max hobbled away. Rented an apartment. Sent for his stuff. That was their big scene—although, in fact, one of their smallest and least original. He thought it was very conventional of her, very Bennington, to object to *Now*. His friends at *Rearview* had said, "You haven't sold out, you haven't sold out. What, Max Jamison sell out?" Did Helen know something they didn't?

He spent a miserable logy evening with Jonathan Briggs, the unworldly editor of *Rearview*, grilling him on these points.

"Look, Max—you have two children I understand . . ."

"You have five."

"Yes, well. That's different. I'm not sure that I haven't sacrificed them. Jonathan Jr. stole a car last week. Courtesy of my idealism about the New York public schools."

"That's a fallacious argument, Jon, I don't have to tell you. Good God, look at the kids in private schools."

"And besides the money, I don't blame you for wanting a larger audience. They'll let you write what you want, won't they?" These old saints didn't really understand anything, so they were very tolerant.

"I can't live with a wife who thinks I'm a sell-out. I can't begin a new job with her on my back."

"I don't blame you."

Jonathan had lived with a black-hearted shrew for thirty years, a woman who complained openly about her husband's weak earning powers, a woman who served California sauterne—and that with a bad grace; but Jonathan didn't blame him. Blame me, go ahead, or I'll pull your eyebrows until they hurt. Max was on his fourth Scotch—the one that should have a goat printed on the glass.

"You *have* to think I'm a sell-out, Jon. Otherwise, *your* life has been a waste of time."

"Not for me, Max. I have a different temperament."

"You can carry a woman on your back?"

"That's right. A big one. I'm not creative. My wife doesn't have to be on my *team*, the way yours does. And I like planning my daughter's school, going fishing with my son. That's why I was shocked about Jonathan Jr. Enjoying your children doesn't seem to help them much."

"It'll work out all right. Kids that age are supposed to be wild."

"Yes, but stealing cars."

I don't want to talk about this. A life of virtue had scattered Jonathan's wits. He couldn't stick to the point worth a damn. Children opened a brand-new vein in Max's neck, something beginning with J. Justin, jugular, Judas priest.

"I feel lousy about leaving the kids, Jon. I just don't know what to do about that."

Jonathan stirred his drink—he was getting stewed himself, out of politeness.

"Nothing could be worse for them than living with parents who despise each other. Right?" said Max.

"Right."

"A father who's treated with naked contempt is worse than no father at all. Confuses the kids."

"Right."

Jonathan, who was treated as fiscally impotent, therefore no man, even in front of guests; Jonathan who was to blame for the furniture, the neighborhood, the poor quality of the vacations; Jonathan, a bowed bleeding ninny, held up to his kids as the ultimate in human weakness—was nodding now like a doll, as Max preached the opposite policy.

"Goddamnit, Jon. Why do you think you have trouble with your son? Because your wife kept him from respecting you all these years, that's why. He has no father to emulate."

Never trust a drunk, even a saintly one. Jonathan seemed to wake from his doze of tolerance. "When your kids grow up perfect, we can talk about that, Max."

"Hey, I'm sorry."

"There is no way of raising kids, repeat, no way at all, that carries a guarantee."

"Yes, I see that. I'm sorry."

The evening ended on this rather sour note, and their relationship had not been quite the same since. No great loss—Briggs was too good for real friendship anyway. Or else not good enough. A prig who had driven his wife and children crazy. But Max had often thought about that last exchange as his own connections with Justin had loosened. You never knew anything about your children—but living with them sometimes gave you the illusion you did. Separation was in some ways a truer condition.

"Max," said Eve. "I'm over here." He gave a start. He had been settling his old problems on her time. Difficult to open a fresh box of emotions with a new friend. However, they would have little problems of their own by and by. For instance, if he cared for her, why had he slept so wolfishly with that campus queen? Critic, review thyself. The old preacher of moral seriousness preached a good game, but had a way of leaving it in the locker room.

"We all get a fixed stare in my business," he explained. "It doesn't mean we aren't attending." Glass and Spangle had dribbled away, and the bar was quiet enough to hear in.

"It isn't that," said Eve. "I wish you wouldn't attend so much. I wish I could split an infinitive with you sometime, or have a really silly discussion."

"You'd like that?"

"Well, not too often. Just once in a while, to prove I still could. Were you always so strict?"

"Yes, ma'am. It's no strain at all. I had two little sisters to practice on, and a father who practiced on me. 'Max—my boy—don't come in the house dangling those participles'—one of those quaint, dry men."

"You've told me about him."

"Let me tell you again, I'm in the mood. The 'where did I go wrong' mood. Bruffin has goaded me into confession. My father must have toilet-trained me himself. 'Now, Max, you hold the paper thus, three strokes up, four down. The way Dr. Johnson did it.' That's how critics are born."

"What about critic's mother?"

"Critic's mother was another story. She made mistakes every time she talked. She hopefully didn't used to be disinterested in whatever transpired—a mess, a hopeless incurable mess. My father never said anything to her. I don't know if they'd fought about it once. I think he corrected us to get at her."

It sounded, in the telling, more freakish than it was. Most people didn't understand that particular temperament of his father's. Compulsiveness doesn't have to be grim. Jamison Sr. had been a half-smiling man, who played croquet in a waistcoat, and took Max to concerts and museums as if commanded to by God. Then home to practice the cello. Max had grown up with the arts, but always with this slight picture-straightening tendency. Courtesy of Dad.

Mr. Jamison looked like Calvin Coolidge and still

worked in the same Boston bank he had started with. He never referred to it—it was just a thing one did, like going to the bathroom. His real life was spent correcting the children's grammar and getting them to Symphony Hall on time. Max thought of him as a New Englander crowded almost into the sea by this big sweaty country. Sometimes he actually seemed to believe he was an Englishman. He was hard on American culture, even the Transcendentalist kind. He thought that Emerson was an old tea cozy and Thoreau the true founder of the *Reader's Digest*. Max was raised on English and French literature; American, if one read it at all, was for entertainment.

They had diverged some place in Max's teens. His father was too slight, his chest was too small, his appreciation too anemic. Max wanted to dominate the arts, ride them like sea-horses. Mr. Jamison was too passive and feminine about it. What was he practicing his cello *for?* Max was growing into a wild man, a roarer. He watched his father humbly scraping alongside his Mozart records, and wanted to smash the cello over the neat gray head and the spanking-clean pink ears.

How could anyone ask so little of life? Max never quite fought with his father, it would have been bad taste, but he treated him with cautious contempt. His mother, vigorous, careless, was the better of the two. Her he argued with, raging and ranting like Thomas Wolfe, and having a huge time. "Mother, for Christsake, isn't there some other way of putting it? Besides 'my feet are *kill*ing me'? Besides 'I have a perfectly *split*ting headache.'"

"What's wrong with that? I see what's wrong with your language, but I don't see what's wrong with mine."

Admirable woman. She drove him crazy, but he thanked her for the swaggering vitality that set him apart from his father, and for his enabling arrogance. And when she wasn't around, as a scratching post, he had his sisters—vague, bored girls, he never saw them now, who had somehow missed the cultural heritage. Sally and Penelope had grown up under the same gentle pedantry as he had, but they hadn't the brains to profit from it. Sally had studied the piano for eight years, making no discernable headway, while Penelope rebelliously had refused to study anything.

Genes take funny bounces. Sally had inherited her father's will to fail and her mother's mental sloppiness. Penelope had done a little better. She had the animal strength to complement her thick wits. A hiker, an habitué of campfires, a bawler of second verses: that was the form her artistic inheritance took. Max alone had worked out right, the right jiggle of X's and Y's. One had to know that about oneself, to amount to anything.

His mother and father took pride in him. They saved his old columns. His father discussed them thoughtfully, on their rare reunions, particularly liking this and that. They were especially pleased when he went to *Now;* were distressed to hear about him and Helen, "just when things were going so well." These were opinions that went with false teeth; Mr. Jamison would not have been pleased with *Now* once upon a time.

"That's enough of that," said Max. "My ration of navel watching."

"Some confession. I must have missed the part where you went wrong," said Eve. "It sounds as if everything worked out fine."

"Yes, it's a habit, making it sound wonderful. I can't tell it any other way. I really thought it was wonderful, until my wife told me otherwise—told me that I was spoiled, from being a little king, that I had actually picked up the worst from my parents rather than the best. Well, you can make up the kind of thing yourself."

Eve frowned. "Do you mind if I say that your wife sounds awful?"

"Not at all," said Max. "Most natural thing in the world. She isn't, though. I'd be the first to know if she was."

"She sounds like your average American ball-cutter to me. Luckily she hadn't cut all the way through. Tough material, I guess."

"You should hear her side of it," said Max, but Eve's remark had excited him, and he didn't want to go on with that stuff. Ex-husbands always made ex-wives sound dreadful, and vice versa, even when they weren't trying. "I'd have to tell you so much more. And even then, you'd have to have been there. She's a good, feminine woman, a joy to live with. It's just that her view of life and mine differ radically. Apollo and Dionysus, if you like, classic versus romantic, whatever your favorite opposites, we occupied them all. It took time to sort this out, that's all."

"All right, have it your way." Eve was warming up too, perhaps. They were ready to try bed again: once again skipping romantic procedure. Maybe people born after 1940 hadn't heard about it.

"If I could prove to myself that she was unintelligent, I would be released of a great burden."

Eve, huddling close to him, although there was plenty of room at the table, said "Hush." He loved her now, of course. That was easy. He wondered what surprises, what delicacies, her body was preparing for him right this minute. He would ravish her like a blind man, gorge and grope and buck like a lion. And then he would look at her eyes and hope it was still there; look again the next morning—closely; to see if he loved her, if lust had crystallized into something solid. So far, though, no sale.

All was as planned, her eyes as questioning as his, her body highly affirmative. He lay beside her in the dark, thinking of the white frame house, as neat as his father's waistcoat. He liked to think about that after making love. And of the garden his father worked in, patiently, for twenty, thirty years, out of duty, like a man shaving his face for work. Mr. Jamison had been assigned this little piece of ground, and it was up to him to keep it from annoying people. "Why do you do it, Father, explain yourself." He had always wanted to ask that in real life, but could never think of a way to put it. His father turned round now, the old smarty-pants, and said, "But, Max, we're both doing the same thing." And giggled, to show he wasn't real. Max always put a little spit on his fantasies. His father was not a weak man, though; a little stiff and constricted, but he could still put you down if necessary.

Max, the gardener, the trimmer of hedges and stuffer

of birds, sat up in bed. Eve lay looking at him with neutral gaze. She was as cool as a critic. Was that what he liked about her? Or were they all like that these days? All the college girls he hadn't paused to notice—taking notes on his course. He might learn something useful from Eve, at that.

13

January and February and March, a bluster of speeches. Major policy address at major journalism school. Functions of criticism, I do declare. Huge convocation, five hundred irreplaceable dollars—you want functions of criticism, big boy, I give you functions of criticism.

There was a youth contingent lounging in back of the hall, the kind of young men who rallied to Cataline with fingers snapping, who drove Juvenal simply wild, who swarm like ants over dead societies of all types; who struck Helen as wonderfully promising. There might be trouble from them by and by.

But, first, the drones must be heard out. "It seems to

me that what Mr. Jamison is saying . . . we don't have that problem in Toledo so far . . . these young writers have no discipline." The youths conveyed barbaric disdain: they would not hesitate to shoot the old men if they thought it would please Che.

Max was drowsily polite with the old men. They had come a long way to learn nothing. They would return to Toledo, muttering "We don't have that problem in Toledo; not just yet; the speaker was very stimulating but he said that we don't have that problem."

At last, youth spoke; a tall, gangling girl already in full squirm. "I mean, all this stuff," she said. "My *God!* What's the point? I've been listening for an hour and a half, and I haven't heard anything yet."

"Is that meant to be a question?"

"Well, yes. I mean, *you* know, what's the point? The most exciting art nowadays just can't be talked about in the old way."

"How should it be talked about?"

"*I* don't know. As experience. As something you feel . . ."

"Yes, well, we try to do that too, you know. Your crowd didn't invent feeling, or anything else. We try to distinguish between real feeling and fake, to tell you, if it comes to that, which nude cellist you should be listening to or what body paint you should be using. Give us your art and we'll criticize it, however incoherent it is."

"Yeah, well you see, that's the thing," said a thin sandy-bearded fellow. "We don't want you to do that any more. We think you just get in the way, with your distinctions and your little adjectives and things. All this verbalizing, you can ruin anything with it. Look at the Beatles. The eggheads got to them and look at them now."

"Is that all?" Max asked stiffly.

"I guess so." The fellow suddenly sat down, as if struck by delayed embarrassment.

"Kids today," piped up someone else, "just don't go for that stuff . . ."

Max gave a sharp bellow. "*You.* You're the one. You're the one who's causing all the trouble. Come out here, and let's have a look at you."

Startled, blinking, pushed by someone, a chubby young man appeared in the center aisle. Tired old heads craned around. Max had himself a victim, if he wanted one.

"I would like you, young man, to ponder very deeply —if pondering is part of your 'thing'—the profound vacuity of your last remark. 'Kids today,' you say. What kids? Everywhere one goes these days, one is threatened, blackmailed, by this phantom, kids today. But when I ask who they are, I am told, well, you know, man, it's like Marshall McLuhan, it's like non-linear.

"Well, I don't want to go into Marshall McLuhan. I might drown in the shallowness. I won't bother you with the figures on books published and sold last year, which indicate that this generation is fairly steeped in print, wallowing, groveling in print, and that today's kids are so linear that they read only the most linear books—histories, biographies, government reports— and never go near those famous French novels that are supposed to speak for them: Robbe-Grillet, etc. . . ."

"Objection," said somebody.

"Overruled," said Max. "I want to finish with this representative youth first. I should like to ask him this. Suppose, sir, that you do have this particular mystic pipeline to today's youth, that you are truly in a position to speak for them, and not just for your lazy self— can you tell me why *I* should throw away a lifetime in the arts, a lifetime of hard-won appreciation and of the most intense pleasure, on the word of some child who has never been there at all? and whose method of persuasion is alternately to grunt and to wriggle?

"Don't misunderstand me, sir. I am not against youth as such. They are wonderfully teachable. But that *they* should be teaching *us;* that we should invest them with oracular powers, read into their shrugs and moans some great gnostic wisdom—this is an American superstition so crass that one scarcely knows where to begin with it."

The old men in the front cheered for the first time, loudly and wildly, to the point of cardiac risk. Max felt green mold forming in the seams of his cheeks, as he led his old men's army over the barricades; hobbling and leering and brandishing their wooden limbs. He didn't want to go on with this argument, he was suddenly sick of it. But he had to conclude.

"I don't want to overstate the case. Youth has a point of view that needs to be heard. But does it need to be heard quite so much? In every lecture hall, some young man or woman, possibly bright, possibly not, it doesn't seem to matter, stands up challengingly as if his very presence were a crushing proposition: and then says nothing. Either he can't or he won't talk. As if speech itself were a corruption handed down by old people.

How many of these kids really know, really feel, and how many are simply making virtues of inarticulateness and the inability to think straight?"

The old men were flushed and happy. Their various pilgrimages were justified. Max by this time loathed his argument. The old fools, their wheelchairs drawn up in a circle, applauded their leader loud and long. "Let's hear it for articulateness! Let's hear it for thinking straight!"

He listened dejectedly to the fat boy's riposte. Why were fat people so touchy? "Your generation has made pretty much of a mess, hasn't it?" he said.

"I wouldn't want to take anything away from Mr. Jamison's experience," interrupted the one with the brown beard, evidently the sage of the outfit, "but that's his experience and not mine. I don't see any point in my repeating his lifetime, step by step, even if I could. It belonged to a particular social situation that doesn't exist any more. The point is that his critical method was devised for the art of his time. It does not apply to mixed media, happenings, or even nouvelle vague cinema."

Max answered mechanically, knowing that it made no difference now. "I wish that you young people knew just a little cultural history. People of my age had come to grips with surrealism before you were born. I, unlike, I venture to say, you, have read Robbe-Grillet and Sarraute, not to mention Heidegger and Sartre. Modern Art has been around for a long time. I am, of course, still baffled by the simple electric light bulb . . ."

Ah, what did they care what he had read, his little list

of names. It made him all the more pathetic. He scooped up his notes and papers. There would be one or two Uncle Tom kids around the platform, thanking him for his illuminating remarks; but the big fish, the ones worth reaching, were already shrugging on out. He could hear their comments, brief, not necessarily unkind. By tomorrow he would be forgotten. "Don't forget me, you little bastards"—it was too late to run after them. "You adorable little shits, of course you're important, but I'm important too. All right? Is that a deal?" Of course not. You can't do business with old men.

Eve had already stopped coming to his talks, at his request. He didn't want in any sense to lecture her. Besides, his public appearances got her excited in the wrong way; he didn't like sleeping with votaries, they were too impersonal.

He tried explaining this to her when he got back to her place. He wanted to make some sort of point to somebody, before retiring. So he said he felt he would like her much better if she stopped admiring him in that particular way. It was like a revivalist preacher trying to calm his wife down after a meeting, so that he could get her excited properly: in himself and not in the Holy Ghost.

Eve, drying her hair, seemed, for once, baffled and hurt. She said, "You're not the Holy Ghost, you're just a critic." The closest to cruel she had ever been with him. "I'm not some sort of wide-eyed girl bowled over by a celebrity, or whatever you are." She rejected him that night, and was very close to tears about it. "I think you're crazy," she said.

Outside of the meetings, though, they had been going to more and more places together, screenings, plays, even a party or two.

His colleagues seemed to know all about it; people he hadn't met began to link their names and nobody ever asked him about his wife any more. The deadly efficiency of gossip had done its work, closing the book on his marriage ("We saw it coming") and preparing now to define his new situation for him. Some night soon, gossip would send over a drunken message to tell him how he was doing.

His own unofficial estimate was that, while it still wasn't the great romance he had hoped for, it had this odd quality about it, that it still could be, if his mind would just get uncluttered. It wasn't Eve's fault. So much junk and crud had accumulated in his head that there was hardly room to move. Cultural refuse, old plots, old characters, theories about life, lines from plays, tags from his own sermons: a warehouse where nothing was ever cleared.

Get rid of it, said Helen. You don't need that old armchair. *What, my precious armchair? Not for the world.* That lamp then. *That lamp? You must be mad.* So, every day, he squeezed in among his spiritual belongings, bored and terrified—that was enough, now. No metaphor should go on for more than two lines. The little buggers got out of hand after that and started to run your life— so he let this one go. But he was restless, he liked to make love after speaking. Failing that, his mind kept churning. Everything was fine with Eve, except that the "thing" wouldn't happen, the bells and the music, the zing-zap of the heartstrings, the golly, Mr. Peabody, I seem to be all thumbs today. Had he worn out his instrument, his inner ear? Old lovers go first in the legs, don't they? He approached passion and fell back. "I almost love you, dar—I mean, dear." Meanwhile, gossip was building a nest for them, with little metal bars on it, creating a context from which it might suddenly be quite painful to tear oneself.

Perhaps that was why she was upset tonight. He replayed his entrance: bursting with talk and self-congratulation and hearty Great Dane kisses, all the worst features of a husband and none of the legal advantages. Then, into bed for his rubdown. O.K., but don't come to depend on it, was Eve's message. You want a geisha, at least take your shoes off. Or something like that.

14

Max had a hangover for visitor's day. He tried to avoid this, but Friday was a great night for parties, and when you were talking well, you hated to leave. He sometimes thought it was the talking that gave him the hangovers.

He listened to the doorbell with heavy-headed dismay. His ears could pick up the sea today without difficulty. This was going to be a vicious afternoon. He wished he didn't have to see Justin today. It was just warm enough to play catch, and he saw himself standing out there among the snow banks, heaving a sodden football which felt like a shot-put, and catching it on the ends of his fingers, which would snap like chalk;

and the cold damp air pressing his skull and wetting his eyes. Max hated sports, but Justin might need them some day.

Helen opened the door and smiled politely. "Max, I want to talk to you."

"What about?"

"The same thing we talked about last week. Remember? I've made definite plans."

"You have?"

"Yes. We'll talk about it when you get back."

So he would have to carry that load with him too, all afternoon, in his groaning head. Give me the boy, then. We'll get going.

Justin straggled into view, looking as if he didn't really want to go anywhere either. Max asked him if he wanted to play ball and he shrugged. Good. No ball. Max hated ball. Zoo? Is the zoo open at this time of year? O.K., no zoo. Is the circus in town by any chance? You might have found out about that, Max, before coming. You might also have dried out in a sauna bath, and been whipped sober by silver birches. But no, the circus is not in town.

So what *would* you like to do? Justin shrugged. Max felt a purple splurge of anger shimmering across his spleen. His patience was not finely tuned. Quills sprang from his spine, and the hair in his nostrils was a snarl of barbed wire.

"Do you want to go look at pictures?"

"No." Justin had enjoyed their one visit to the Metropolitan Museum, chuckling over the nudes, etc., but had declined to go back.

"We've seen all the children's movies. Anyway, we can't keep on going to movies indefinitely. We'll both go mad."

Justin looked away. He wants me to leave, thought Max, panicking. His mother's been getting at him. Wait, I'll offer him something. Something made of chocolate. No, I won't. The kid is already spoiled rotten. That's why he doesn't want to go anywhere.

Charlie poked his head out the living-room door, and jerked it back.

"Hi, Charlie. How's the boy?"

"I'm fine."

"That's good." Max didn't know how many words Charlie knew by this time, or what you talked to him about.

"You want to come out with us?"

Charlie nodded. OhmyGod—what were they going to do now? No museum would have them; Charlie could dismantle the best of them in five minutes. Charlie was one of the inspired wreckers of all time—frenzied, yet methodical.

"I'm going out, I'm going out," he piped.

"I don't want to go anywhere with *him*," said Justin.

"Oh, come on now," said Max foolishly. "He's your brother."

"He stinks."

Max felt the hungover rage again, ripping across his vitals. "You'll do what you're told," he said. "And you'll do it on the double."

Justin looked indecisive. Max was now about to whack him and he knew it. He frowned over the problem, and then burst into tears. OhmyGod again, thought Max. Tears in the morning, shepherds take warning. "Go get your things," he said gently, patting Justin on the shoulder.

Once-a-week discipline was impossible. You had to re-draft the whole legal code every Saturday. Helen was old-fashioned permissive—a system guaranteed, in Max's eyes, to produce a race of sullen slobs. Now that Max was gone, she spent the whole week softening and weakening Justin. You could see that some of the sensitiveness had left his face already—that look of awe and gratitude and, let's face it, just a touch of fear: a sense that the world presented certain difficulties. All that going, gone.

Notes: The dull brutish faces of the kids who didn't realize this. Fear forms finer features. Courage, a failure of imagination. Work into big youth piece. *Now* will love it, unfortunately.

"Let's go to the candy store," said Justin, fully recovered.

"All right." I frightened you, now I give you candy. O.K.?

They bought several chocolate bars apiece and then headed for Central Park to enjoy them and to scamper through the mud. They located a children's playground, and Charlie found a sawed-off slide he could master, and handed over his chocolate for Max to hold. Justin, however, sampled all the play objects and found nothing to his taste. "This place is drippy. Let's go."

"Why? Where?" Max asked helplessly.

"I don't know. Any place. This place stinks."

"Charlie's having a good time."

"Yeah. He's a baby. This place is for babies."

"Oh, I see."

Max decided to stay anyway, mainly because he could think of nothing better. Justin went peevishly and sat on a bench, with his back turned. Charlie was absorbed in his twentieth-or-so slide. No problems about him. He would slide until his ass wore away.

Max went over to Justin and tried to strike up a conversation, but it was no go. After a few minutes of gloom and stutter, Justin said, "Let's get something to eat."

"But you've still got a candy bar."

"It stinks. I want something else."

"That's ridiculous, Justin. You can't spend the whole day eating."

"I want something to eat."

"You can't have it. I'm sorry."

"You never get me anything."

"*What?*"

"Never get me anything I want."

Max couldn't help it. He was absolutely disgusted with the boy. Justin's face was set in a fanatical pout. What are you doing to him, Helen? This fine boy?

Justin left the bench and walked jauntily toward the swings. A toddler in a snow suit was doing his best to urge the swing into the air, leaning back on the seat and puttering with his feet. Justin went up behind him and pushed the kid off. The child floundered like a hockey goalie in his thick wrappings, and squalled dementedly. My God. Max looked on in frozen horror. Justin peeked back, over his shoulder, defiant and deeply frightened. Then he boarded the swing himself.

Max sat for a while with his head in his hands, holding it like a large rock. Helen, what have you done? What do you mean, what have *I* done? what have *you* done is more like it. Since I left . . . yes, but who buys him candy? I only see him once a week. I can't help that. Yes but yes but.

You're ruining him, Max. He came to my room last night, Max, crying his heart out. And he climbed into bed and he said why did Daddy leave? and then he said, I hate Daddy. Was that what Helen would say?

The picture was intolerable, even though he'd made it all up himself. A little boy wandering in a corridor at night searching for his father. Max, how did you let this happen? What did you suppose you were doing, at any one point? His brain would burst from melancholy, scatter into black shards. Maybe, he thought desperately, rapprochement with Helen was still in the cards. Go back to having his balls kicked in. Leave Eve, still wondering. Leave his lousy, sour-smelling freedom. To save Justin and keep him from pushing little kids off swings.

He had at least half made up his mind, and he decided to get them all back early, so he could feel out Helen. He didn't want to be theatrical, tell her how much he'd learned and suffered, but simply to talk about Justin and what was best for him. He wondered what it was that Helen wanted to talk about—possibly the same thing, only the other way around.

Justin walked briskly now, as if he wanted this meeting too; or as if he just wanted to get home. Charlie was attached to his slide, whumping gleefully into the cold sand, and pretending not to hear Max. So he had to be yanked away and hoisted bawling homeward.

I've got to see more of the boys, not less. I can master this tendency to give them gifts. If I see them, say, Saturdays and alternate Sundays and midweek afternoons, I'll get used to them, and the bribery will cease. And perhaps we can synchronize our methods a little better. "Oh, for Godsake, Charlie, it's only a slide." But Charlie was still wailing and muttering when they got to the apartment. "I want my mommy, I hate my daddy," stuff of that sort.

Helen gathered them in with a sweeping motion. "Max, I've got a surprise— What's the matter with Charlie?" The boy had lashed himself to her knees and was shrieking into her red skirt.

"He wanted to go on sliding. Till Christmas of next year. What's your surprise?"

It wasn't a great moment to bring up seeing more of the boys. Justin had gone straight to his room and shut the door. Charlie was beyond his comprehension. What the hell had Max done wrong, to cause this scene of rout?

"That's all right, dear. Daddy had to bring you home. You can go sliding tomorrow."

Not with me, you don't. Max never wanted to go near that slide again. He shifted his feet. Helen was slightly blocking his path, as if she didn't want him to come in.

"Can we sit down a minute?"

"That's what I want to talk about. I mean there's someone inside I want you to meet."

"Yeah? Who's that?"

"Let me explain. He's a wonderful man—"

"Oh, I see." The hammer crashed slowly into his eyes. "One of those."

"His name is Gene Mungo and he paints."

"Oh Christ, you're kidding, aren't you? Gene Mungo? He's an idiot."

"We differ. Just let's let it go at that. I want to go and live with him. So, do you want to meet him or not?"

"Oh hell, I've met Gene Mungo. I've even tried to talk to him. Believe me, it wasn't easy."

"Words aren't his specialty."

"I'll say they're not. They're not even one of his side dishes."

"Gene is outside your world, your little word-world, absolutely beyond your power to understand. It doesn't matter. Do you want to say hello anyway?"

"Not much. What would be the use? I'd have to dance it out for him. Hey, wait a minute"—these Eve Arden wisecracks were just the first quick accumulation of bile. They didn't represent his position. Helen had taken a couple of disgusted steps away. "Where will you be taking the boys?"

"We'll see. Somewhere on the New England coast, I expect. Maine possibly. Gene does his best work up there."

"You mean he goes all that way to paint Daddy's boots at sunrise, or whatever you call that crap?"

"Have you got anything serious you'd like to say?"

"Yes, of course I have. How the hell am I going to visit the kids on the coast of Maine? My work is in New York, you know that."

"I'm sorry, Max. I don't think the present set-up is too wonderful for the boys. Look at today, for instance . . ."

"You mean to tell me you never have any trouble with the boys? That every day is perfect?"

"I didn't say that. I say that you unsettle them, that's all. Anyway, there's no point arguing about it. They'll be happier in the country. Gene is wonderful in the country, he can teach them how life works."

Since when were you so hot on the country, he wanted to ask. Helen was born and raised in Indianapolis. But this was a petty debating point, and at that he might lose it. They probably had great botanical gardens in Indianapolis. What he wanted to rage at was the very notion of this disorganized baboon fathering his boys.

"Look, I give them something, don't I, Helen? I know you have your private case against me, I understand that and wouldn't disturb it for the world. But taking me at my worst reading . . ."

"You'll see them in the summer, if you still want to."

"And meanwhile, that clown will have been working them over all year, showing them the miracle that we call a robin's egg, the wondrous filaments of the chestnut leaf."

"That wouldn't be such a bad program, if you omitted the sarcasm."

"Look, Helen, *look*. He isn't even a good artist. He's a damn fraud. He can't even draw an apple."

"You think that's important."

"You're damn right it's important. I don't want my sons raised by a mountebank. How can they learn truth and beauty from a man who desecrates both every time he puts his brush between his toes?"

"I don't happen to agree with you at all. I'll have to show you some of Gene's still-lifes sometime. But leaving that aside—how can you approach a thing like this as an art critic? Have you no other standards at all of judging a man?"

"I certainly have. But I'd rather not even go into those, if we're talking about Mungo. The guy is a complete pig, for openers—a lecher, a hophead, he'll have the kids smoking pot under the porch within a year . . ."

"I've been trying to keep my temper, Max. So I'll just say it once and simply. I love Gene, and I'd just as soon you didn't talk about him any more. It doesn't help your cause, believe me. I happen to think he has one quality that makes up for everything, the one quality that you lack. He loves life. He embraces it. He doesn't have it mediated for him, he doesn't have it strained and filtered and bottled, he doesn't think words are a substitute for it . . ."

"I thought he had it mediated for him through pot and acid a good deal of the time."

"Those things enhance it. That's why you despise them so much. But we don't want to have that old argument again, do we?"

No, we don't. Max had been wasting his time, beating his fists on the cage. No one cared, no one listened. He was such a convincing man, such a good talker. But those qualities counted against him now; they were precisely what was wrong with him. He could argue no further, with the young people, with his wife, because his ability to win arguments was what made him so pathetic and irrelevant to them.

"I'll have to oppose this," he said.

"You'll have a hard time. You'll be getting a thing from my lawyer in a few days, telling you just how hard. I think Gene has some money, not that we need it."

She could think linearly when it suited her purposes, this apostle of the new age. Max hadn't studied the legal angles, but he supposed she was right. Anyway, he didn't want to tear the children apart in a court fight. If Helen was hell-bent on going, there probably wasn't much he could do.

"I'll talk to you later," he mumbled.

"I'm sorry, Max." She closed the door quietly. She gave him more credit than some, allowed that he had feelings, twisted but real enough.

Well, at least he had been spared another view of Gene Mungo. The thought of this dirty, squalid man sprawled between his wife's legs gave him the shakes. My God, what had happened to her? This wasn't some saint, some wild-eyed celebrator of life she had discovered, but a mangy two-bit art hustler, the kind who had debauched the whole New York scene. *Mungo couldn't even paint.* I was at least a good critic.

The pain drenched him slowly as he walked. He supposed he was going home, some place down there anyway. What a step down in class for Helen. Couldn't she see that? Couldn't she tell counterfeit talent, counterfeit vitality when she saw it? He knew his years with her had been wasted, but not as wasted as that. She had less taste, less sense than when she came in. And this *life* business—that fuzzed-up pothead drooling over some daisy he couldn't even name. I, Max Jamison, love life as much as he does. I have walked with Helen through the woods, speechless, strangled with wonder. She knows that. I haven't done it lately. Who has? Things slip away. I must get back to it. Take the boys somewhere . . .

Take the boys. The boys whom he had had such a wretched time with today. That was something quite beyond him. He loved them, but they cried and complained, as if some ugly old man was kissing them. They feared his hands and his breath. Don't let that man touch me. I sing a funny song and they scream with fear.

Every possibility must be considered by the well-ordered critic. Maybe Helen was right. Maybe he should get out of their lives, remove his shadow. They could scarcely be more miserable without him. And his vaunted influence on their minds and tastes seemed to be counter-productive. As it was on Helen, as it was on everybody.

Of course, your work is influential, very, oh yes. Mr. Jamison has taught the natives to wear trousers and tell time. He has taught them standards. For a moment, the plating of irony cracked, and he saw his life as completely, irreparably useless. But that was sentimental, of course. The sentimentality of honesty. The self-indulgence of despair. Despair and insanity were attractive but basically frivolous escapes. Oh Helen, I've failed; oh Helen, forgive me.

He decided to go see Eve, and try to rebuild his tissues. After a woman who thought you were awful, it

137

was only fair to see one who thought you were great. Once you saw that they were both correct, you were a wise man, perhaps. Or a dithering schizoid. It also occurred to him that he had reached a point with Eve— the gossips and Max-watchers would confirm this— where he might consider introducing Eve to the children. He hadn't wanted to upset them with a stream of strange women, but Eve looked as if she might last a while. The gossips and the theorists would bear this out. The kids wouldn't like her at first, any more than they liked pickles or oysters or anything new and complicated. They would chant "I hate her, I hate her. Are you going to marry her?" It would be a trial.

On the other hand, Eve would help him through the visiting afternoons, would know how to cajole them from slides, divert them from chocolate. Also, sing funny songs to them that didn't come out sounding vaguely sinister, hug them without hurting, remember their gloves.

He had forgotten for a moment that Helen was going away, and that visitation Saturdays might soon be over for good. Could this be? What court would allow Gene Mungo in the same house with a child? He'd have to look into that on Monday. Meanwhile, he kept walking toward Eve's, for now.

15

Unhappy families are the ones that are all alike. Tolstoy had got it all wrong. He should start his whole book over again. Max had listened to the lonely whine of the divorcee so often; and here he was in precisely the same bag, making the exact same noises. It would probably be the height of affectation to alter the script, to have a really different kind of divorce.

"I'm sorry I'm boring you with all this," he said to Eve. "I usually keep these things to myself. Which is part of my trouble, according to Helen. Buttoned up to the chin, says she."

"I'm not bored," Eve said. "If you want to talk."

"I don't especially. I thought I'd try it and see. But it doesn't make any difference. Talk, not talk."

Eve shrugged. "Well, do what you like," she said.

He suddenly wanted to say, you bore me. But that wouldn't have been quite accurate. He wanted somehow to settle things quickly, get some conclusive message to both his women and go to bed on it. Talk was too slow a medium.

Eve was sitting across from him, holding a glass between her knees. She was wearing Bermuda shorts, scarcely one of his favorite items. Why don't you make that little extra effort and become truly first-rate? He must settle this quickly. The answer to his problem clearly involved Eve. If he were to set up house with her right away, he would have a base from which to fight for his children. Helen had doubtless committed adultery with George Dirty, leaving a trail of telltale grime like a chimney sweep's across the sheets; he could now sue her, reclaim his children, and raise them properly, indoors.

Eve was frowning helplessly. Max realized that he had just been sitting staring at her. Wearing her down.

"Do you like children?"

"I don't know. Which children?"

"Other people's."

"That's the only kind I know, so far."

"Don't be funny, please. I'm not in the mood."

"If you mean"—and she said this so casually that he didn't realize its finality—"would I be interested in looking after yours, I'm afraid the answer is no."

"What do you mean? Why did you say that?"

"I thought it might come up."

"Couldn't you have waited?" He shook his head. "I don't know what to say next. You've answered a ques-

140

tion I haven't even asked." He was suddenly disgusted. "What do you mean, you wouldn't look after my children?"

My God, thin-faced and empty like the rest of them. What did they think they were doing? What was the point of these people?

"I'm not ready for children yet, Max. There are too many things I want to do first."

Ah so? What things? Take another course, study ballet theory under Professor Steingut, screw a few Great Minds. You think you'll be ready for children after that? You won't, you know. You'll be terrified of them. You'll take them to psychiatrists every time they sneeze. You'll take more courses. You'll study child psychology under Professor Quakenbush. Why can't you see all that?

"I thought I'd make it clear, so there were no misunderstandings later."

Will no one help me with my children, thought Max desperately. Nobody took this question very seriously except him. Why did he care so much? He had no special plans for them, didn't know what to do with them on Saturday afternoons. So why wouldn't he let them go? Instead of brooding around them like some great farm dog?

"You're not angry, are you, Max?"

"No. I just wasn't ready. I wish you'd waited until the conversation had reached that point."

She came over and put her arm around him, but for once he didn't respond. If you don't want my children, you don't want me. That was the only difference that really stood up between a love affair and a quick lay.

Looking for magic in her eyes—what foolishness! Do you want the kids or don't you, was the question he should have asked all along.

She returned to her seat. She looked upset for a second, which didn't make any sense at all.

"I'm sorry, I shouldn't have brought it up. It was nothing personal about your children, of course—oh, what's the use of saying that? I'm just sorry, that's all."

"Yes, so am I."

She looked embarrassed. "Don't you think it might be for the best, Max? Do you really see yourself as a full-time father?"

"Sure. Why not?"

"I don't know. You don't seem like the type."

She, too, saw him as a glacial, disembodied brain. A face carved on a mountainside. How unjust you're all being. *I* know I'm not like that. It is true that my work requires a certain hardness. Diamond cutting is like that. But off-duty, I am *all right*.

"I am sure your children are quite wonderful," said Eve.

"Yeah, yeah. Captivating little beggars. The one with the depressed cranium is especially enchanting."

"Why do you say that? What's the matter?"

"You don't give a damn about my children, so let's not go on about them, shall we?"

"It isn't like that."

Homicidal rage was the order of the year. He doused it quickly with critical method. In what sense did she love him if she wouldn't put up with his children? Eros, agape, courtly wish-need, what is it to be? He looked around the apartment for what he knew was to be the last time. No sense wasting her time.

She probably didn't grasp this. In her eyes, she had expressed a simple difference of taste. She was ready now for dinner plans. Bland, intelligent, never quite first-rate. He despised her.

The temptation was to express this in marble words that would sit in her mind forever, and some day become clear to her, and constitute his final lesson. But he was so heartsick about his own life that he could hardly speak at all. He stood up like a drunk. I cannot go on like this. Those were the words for now. He must remember them well. He shook his head solemnly at Eve and said good night. Wonder what she makes of that, he asked himself on the stairs. Her blank eyes followed him home, growing blanker with every step.

part three

16

And now the running battle with irony was on. Irony was the thing that must go, if anything was to change. Yet he found himself posing the question with irony. To wit: that Saturday night was a good time to start changing your life. If you did it with the speed of Scrooge, you could be all straightened out by Monday and no one the wiser.

Facetiousness shook him like ague. What were the standard ways of losing your old self? Start with the pleasant ones. Depravity, defilement were ever popular. Getting drunk, dissolving through bright-colored rooms, gay bars, dyke bars, transvestite propositions, down into the grayer tones, until the kaleidoscope straightens and shakes you out on the street. At the feet of some cop. Secondary characteristics: face, eyes blurring, brain silting up, foul taste, self-contempt. "Arrest me, officer, I am the lowest of men." Very popular indeed a few years ago, but rather cornball now. Too predictable. What actually happened was that you wound up tottering in front of some men's-room mirror saying, Well you certainly made a chump of yourself tonight, Jamison. Self-loss had to include more surprises than that.

How about something a little more contemporary—getting high on drugs, rising instead of falling? Battling the wily teenager, coming to grips with the dreaded hippie? Jamison in Night Town, dancing to twitching lights and brain-cracking music. White-faces grinning in a circle. Old man shaking with palsy to a Watusi beat. Old man dancing himself to death while tribe looks on. Head aching, eyes running now: not losing self, but confirming it. To let himself be laughed at for one whole evening: what crud that would scrape away.

The worst of it was that he knew his mind would still work the old way, under whatever weight of marijuana or booze. He had trained it to. It only knew the one way of working. E.g., instead of dismantling himself in front of some impassive bartender, he would wind up arguing with the man about his favorite movie; or he would sit there silently and think about bartenders; or about teenagers; or about Max Jamison thinking.

He was in love with the way his mind worked, and he was sick of the way his mind worked. The first thing that struck you about it, wasn't it, was the blinding clarity, like a Spanish town at high noon. No shade anywhere. Yet not altogether lacking in subtlety. Very fine filigree work in the church. This was the mind they were asking him to blow.

He sat on his bed, leaning his weight on his hands. Exhaustion was another thing you could do. Walk all night, alongside silvery rivers, dank canals, inland waterways, until you arrived in Schenectady, all gray and wasted. This man does not remember his name. Knows the names of all Greta Garbo's movies, but does not remember his own name. Claims to be George Jean Nathan, in his more lucid moments.

Hah. No exhaustion, no heat of day or shock of battle could keep Max Jamison from remembering his own name. That was the whole point. He could spot "Max Jamison" in a forest of words, hear it in the roar of the crowd. He *was* his name, in a way that non-writers could never understand. Its appearance above an article meant that he was about to read something dazzling. A reference to it in someone else's writing meant an automatic quickening of interest, the invasion of a marvelous fresh point of view. A slur on it was like an insult to Helen of Troy, never to be forgotten.

He had a hunch that if he could forget his name, the rest would slip away without effort. But a writer and his name are not easily parted. On his deathbed, where a decent man would be calling on the saints, Jamison would be mumbling his own name faster and faster— not with one of your peaceful smiles either, but feverishly, to insure the maximum of mentions before closing shop; his name, like the pennies on a dead man's eyes, would be useful coin in the next world.

We exaggerate, do we not, Max. The name was just another chain on his leg that had to be patiently filed through. The name and the identity. Be very clear about this. He could not go on as he was. He could not present the old Max to another woman. He could not go through the obscene ritual of giving and receiving, first fascination, then disgust, and retiring to his mirror and falling in love all over again. You could argue whether his life up to now had been wasted (he thought not, but it wasn't important). But it certainly would be if he could urge it no further forward than this.

Did he *have* to go on repeating himself? Was that what personality meant? There must be many people who just never noticed they were repeating themselves. His sisters, for instance. But "Know thyself" was the name of Jamison's racket; he must poke and prod like Oedipus until all was unstuck. In spite of all Sophocles had told him, he had supposed he was *choosing* to act like Max Jamison: because he liked the way Max Jamison acted. Fat choice he had had. Putting your eyes out with a hot poker was supposed to change your luck. But even then he saw an endless sequence of Eves and Helens—girls that he would disappoint and girls that would disappoint him. It was sewn into the lining of Jamison's personality that he would flunk a certain number of women for their human deficiencies; but that others would flunk him for his, and because he gave the same course year after year. The problems were not disconnected, of course. Flunk or be flunked. Race you, professor.

The regular American thing would be simply to become a nice guy. Have you noticed how Jamison has mellowed? But there were ugly precedents for that. Critics who mellowed lost their teeth and never got them back. Fritz Cunningham was an outstanding example. Killer Fritz, readers would moan for him to stop. "Don't hit that play any more, you brute," they screamed. But when he did stop, and after they got over their first delight at his conversion, they began to say, Have you noticed how dull Fritz has gotten? Then, when he tried to resume his old ways, he could not recapture his bite, his fangs were false and loose.

And even a regular human being who became a nice guy was usually a sorry sight, like a reformed alcoholic, gray, wistful, played out; worse, flabby and weak as a kitten; and finally, if one could ever arouse him, deeply resentful. Becoming a nice guy was a weasely evasion—no change of self was involved, just a closing down of certain outlets, a contraction. The enclavement theory of personality. Max might have to resort to it yet, to end his last days in peace; with a woman he would simply not permit himself to loathe. But first he intended to blow the works—if he still could.

How about some kind of mysticism? He supposed that some brands were better than others. The correspondence-course ones—Zen, yoga—well, how could you face your friends? The classic brands—Hinduism, old-line Buddhism—were all right if you weighed ninety pounds and had the bones of a bird. But you could not really separate religion from culture, and he knew it. It was what you ate and how you dressed and what language you used. An American Buddhist was ridiculous. An American who cultivated the best from all the world's religions was a simpering toady.

It seemed he had burned most of the bridges that led away from his current personality. That was why he loved it so. Christianity? Ah, Christianity. That old thing. All the same, he might try a retreat in a monastery sometime. Contemplation should be left to the professionals. If he spent three days with his own thoughts he would become more and not less himself. He didn't really have thoughts any more, only sodden doubts and anxieties, which bound him like heavy wet bandages, with his name embossed on them in shit. Better to listen to some old fool chanting about how they crossed the Red Sea and made a perfect fool of Pharaoh, and about gardens of myrrh and aloes, and the cedars of Lebanon. Get a fellow's mind off things.

Do not be put off by the irony, gentlemen. It is just a question of style. I am really a very serious man. I have fallen into certain habits. Style—good Lord, would that have to go, too? The harsh short sentences (what is the sound of one tooth biting?). The graceful longer ones. Languor and lazy amusement. Majesty and moral indignation. The whole bright colored bag of tricks.

—But gosh, Mr. Jamison, sir—those aren't tricks, are they? I mean, they sound so real, when you do them.

—Well, I don't like to break your heart, honey, but of course they're tricks. What do you suppose writing is all about? Come to think of it, I'm not really Max Jamison—

And with that, he ripped off his rubber nose and flung it into the audience. "You see, my dear, I am really—" But she had already wandered away, and in a moment the theater was empty. Nobody cared who he really was.

Yeah, Fat Lady, how about that one? How was he going to make a living if he changed his style? It was enough act of faith to presume that there was a real self under his big bad one; but to suppose there was another style under there as well—that was madness. Consider, once again, Fritz Cunningham, the prototype of the writer who monkeys with change. Fritz had altered his style, under pressure of psychoanalysis, but the result had been sheer disintegration. Max could picture the doctor saying, "Ja, you are showing off here, you are kissing your big toe there . . . and this is a flat lie," until all color, all idiosyncrasy were gone. It is really rather neurotic to try to avoid clichés, Herr Jamison: an attempt to set yourself apart from your peers.

A really good spiritual director would probably tell him to give up writing altogether. It was all tied in with his character and was doomed to the same repetitions, the same cycle of narcissism and contempt. You'll never get well if you go on writing, little Hans Jamison.

He went to the kitchen and yanked an apple out of the icebox. Returned to the bed and began to chew it, over the wastebasket. Getting sick of one's style was old stuff for writers. At least it proved you had one. Some juice ran down his sleeve. He could see himself compromising on all this. Remaining the same in his work, and changing himself in his free time. A lot of people did it that way. Honestly.

Mahatma Gandhi and Albert Schweitzer had a good laugh at this point. You Americans! You want to do something about that bag of liquid cement you call a soul—and you want to do it in your spare time. Ho, ho, ho.

Sorry, fellows. I understand that it should be the work of a lifetime and that it involves, at the very least, leaving town. But I have an opening Monday and a deadline Tuesday and a lecture date, and Helen's going to want twice as much money to support that sponging leper of hers—love of life comes high. And I want to see the kids. And, well, just look at that calendar, will you?

He threw the core into a nest of screening notices. Didn't know what to do, really. He had seen through so many people's spiritual efforts, seen through and mocked every single choice he could think of now. He must simply roll out the list again and see if he'd missed anything. The temptation was to say, Well, you certainly took a good hard look at yourself, didn't you, Max, and go to sleep on it. But then he thought back to the afternoon, the two women, Helen and Eve, the pillars that bounded his present world, and he knew that he mustn't slide into facetiousness or irony or fatty tolerance, but must take some hard road out of here.

So he started to think, more slowly this time, of the world of drugs and prayer and of various styles in solitude. Max Jamison was really an old man coated in sand, with a raven on his wrist. He sat at the floor of his cave, and another old man with a cowl, and no face, came up and said, "Sweep away the old man, sweep away the sand, and think about what's left. That's contemplation for you, sonny."

Blah, what a burner on you, Jamison. Any high-school philosophy major could tell you what you're doing wrong. You're using the soul of Max Jamison to change the soul of Max Jamison. The instrument *delicti* to change the instrument *quasi nisi*. Fat chance, fellow.

Next he ran through all the advice he had received from the nation's playwrights on how to live. All the fags and whiners, the promising Negroes and the brutally candid Englishmen, who had undertaken his instruction for the last few years. And he thought, what a load of crap it had all been, what a sack of sophistries. And even when real wisdom popped up, his mind did something peculiar to it, known as criticism, which rendered it sterile and safe for the public.

What about the ideas he had learned in college, with his mind like a switchblade and the zest for learning that Dad or someone had imbued him with, what about those ideas, huh? Irony had killed them all. One by one. Or they had killed each other, Sartre killing Freud, Max killing Sartre—oh, always something else would come along shortly, but just behind that, the knife. Records are made to be broken. I used to be profound once, honestly. Then Mother died, and I had to give it up.

"If you would just forget those words, man, and listen to your body"—he received advice by mail, too, advice by air and sea and every means known to man of carrying advice. All rushing help to Max. Forget words—easy for you to say, Ellie Watkins of Flagstaff, Arizona, who never knew them. Ask Casals to throw away his cello and listen to his body, and see what his answer is.

But what a waste of time anyway, advising a critic. For years, we are paid to take a position, like bare-knuckle champions; and you cannot slip your advice to us swiftly enough to keep us from flying into our stance and clobbering you. Before you have choked out your pitiable comments about forgetting words, I will have told you of the role of language, of how it is not some extra to humanity but the precondition of humanity, and—blah de blah-blah. I bore myself. I don't know whether I believe it any more, or even what I mean by it. But those are the things I say.

I can't help it. Max said these words out loud. There must be some way of changing, some blinding pain, tearing of skin, wearing down of brain. Some wild obliterating scream. On impulse, to make some sort of gesture in that direction, Max got off the bed and lay on the hard floor for a minute in his shirt sleeves. And felt like a damn fool.

17

Max woke on Sunday with a stiff neck and a kink in his spine, prepared to resume the business of contemplation. But first he had a long review to write, due in by Monday. If his contemplation could reach the point, by nightfall, of telling him to screw the review, all reviewing, he could forget it right now. But how can you tell what contemplation is going to say? You mustn't influence the Ouija board. It might say, your place is by your typewriter, Jamison, doing your humble tasks. And then he would be one review in the hole.

So he fished for paper and stuffed it distastefully into the typewriter and rolled it, white, blank, and stupid, into position. He would have to change himself within the context of his profession. Nothing spectacular, no tricks, no retreats; just staying on the job, the way most people had to do it. Waiting for junior's braces to come off.

His fingers crept to their allotted posts on the keyboard. But as he typed the first word he saw that he was still quite nauseated with his own thoughts. He could not stand what he was about to say. This was the same mind that had dismembered two marriages, and all those friendships, the mind that the children hated and feared—he thought of the scabrous Mungo playing with them even now. Happy urchin smiles as the suppurating hand riffled their hair. Mungo pushing them on the swings, bounding around the sandbox, roaring down the slide with a child on each head. My God, to build a family and hand it over to Gene Mungo.

Max decided to get away from his own consciousness before the monster with the bone through his head came scampering out of the long grass to crush him to bran mash. His first thought was to call Eve. Three rings and the French maid answers, "Madame is not 'ere, you son of a bitch." "Eve, Eve, I know it's you." Click. All the women he knew lay stripped and gutted by the roadside, like Puerto Rican automobiles. The trail of smoking, exhausted women led at last to the mansion with the broken windows. And there in the old ballroom—why, upon my soul, it's old Colonel Jamison still leading the quadrille, by George. Say—how about going to one of the art museums and picking something up? A dose of the King's itch, perhaps.

Salvation through work. This piece of paper here, let's cover it in pus and old sores. Crawling and maggoty from contact with Max Jamison's mind. Oh yes, a fine, sensitive mind; but under that satin suit, the smell is quite horrible, you know. Strong women faint when he takes it off. Yes, fact.

Salvation through women. The class of '82 will be called to order, please. Pan to this old crow of a schoolmaster, living on through his pupils. Mr. Chips celebrating his 100th birthday with glass eyes glistening. Helen, ace pupil, lying next to Mungo, the bronze monkey, pays an unsolicited tribute. "Max? Oh, I learned a lot from Max." "Did you really?" "Oh yes. He's a very clever man. Limited, stiff. More than a little bit dead, in fact. But he taught me about standards, their cure and avoidance. That's what I love about you, Gene, baby." You're making this up, Max. Well, of course I am. But just listen to this part. "Gene, you're, I don't know, so disgusting, so loathesome—"

Lessons for all. Eve Sample, we're conducting a survey. What did you learn from Max Jamison? "Max who? Oh yes, Max Jamison. Well, like Helen here I learned about moral attitudes, standards, the natural law. I learned that a woman is supposed to be first an earthmother, second a chum. She should be willing to embrace a man's children sight unseen and give up any pretensions to a life of her own." Oh, come on, that isn't fair. It isn't even well put—Look, whose dialogue is this, Jamison? Shut up and listen. "I learned how a man who does nothing for anybody, whose life is the last word in artifice and sterility, can still demand of his women that they be warm and natural . . ."

He yawned. So much for salvation through women. They all used the same clichés, at least when he was running the sound track. Back to work, then—leaving religion and philosophy for night thoughts. Not the wonders of nature, of growing things, but the pale white moon was his setting for that. He decided, just as an exercise, to see if he could write a piece with no irony in it at all, no Jamison point of view. Plain, rinsed words.

"Last week a new play opened at the Martin Beck"— it gave him the green shudders; he shook like a man with the plague. "Walton Flanders gave his usual fine performance. Mary Seth Edwards, long the first lady of our stage, has contributed another in her long series of unparalleled contributions to our long indebted to Mary Seth Edwards, deservedly called the first lady of our contributions." He thought about the seductions of dullness, the discipline it must take never to say anything clever or interesting, and the tingling satisfaction afterwards. A succulent perversion, practiced widely in back of the House of Commons.

He couldn't think of anything else to say. Somehow he had lost the middle ground between wit and swooning cliché. Was *Now* to blame for this? Had they forced him to make the one joke too many? Or did it go back further than that?

Max's earlier writing had actually been rather too serious. He was not a humorous man. Even now, racked with humor, he was not amused.

"According to eyewitness reports, Max Jamison saw a joke at exactly midday of May 15, the date of the last solar eclipse." His father had not told him about jokes. Culture, pleasantness, good humor, yes. But not actual jokes. They would have seemed like a breach of taste.

In high school, Max developed a line of harsh banter, as a blunt defensive weapon; but he was physically unable to laugh at what were known as jokes. He learned about wit from his reading, plays on words and such; even his father liked a good pun occasionally. By his second year at college, Max was able to make jokes that actually counted as jokes, among a few sympathetic friends.

The birth of a wit. Slowly, largely unconsciously, Max brought his dry, humorless jesting into line with middle-brow taste, until his wisecracks were their wisecracks. He didn't think, even now, that he was amused in the same way as they were. But it was like very good plastic surgery, indistinguishable from the real thing.

"Max saw his first joke"—a bad day all around. Like so many late converts, he had fallen with galumphing ardor on his new discovery. He began making jokes all over the place. People marveled at his deadpan delivery, always the mark of your true comic: not understanding that it was because he was not amused, in their sense, at all. He hardly knew how to make the motions of laughter.

He had sensed that in educated America, humor was the number 1 language, for criticism, passion, even cooking: and he set about learning it with grim intelligence. Until he was among the best, far ahead of the naturals and kibitzers. Until it was his actual trademark, dyed into his hide, and he could not write two lines without resorting to it.

Ah Max, you slay me with your theories. That's an ingenious account you have just given of Jamison on humor, but much too schematic and lifeless. Two and a half stars. *Frankly, I didn't believe a word of it, Max.* Oh, I don't know. The part about my father was interesting. Also, I believe I have most of the dates right.

Meanwhile, he was getting nowhere with his piece. It was not true that he couldn't write without irony; he could write with indignation; he could write with tenderness. The truth was that right now he did not feel like writing at all. After last night, he did not feel in shape to criticize anyone. He wasn't going to show off by cringing or by leaking humility and compassion. But he could not in conscience put anybody down either, not from where he stood.

He took a walk instead on the East Side, which seemed to be in Lenten mourning. For the death of their famous corn god. With his women gone, and his children, Max felt like sharing their grief in his own way. Pity about their corn god. He felt, though he resisted the word, lonely. Not free, those days were long gone. Lonely.

Tonight, one of the numerous critics' circles to which he belonged was meeting and he thought, I'll go to that, I'll see how the others are doing. Meanwhile he rambled aimlessly down Madison Avenue. Beauty shops closed tight as a drum. Art galleries. Vanity showings for rich ladies with one leg shorter than the other. A ridiculous, affected avenue. Better the featurelessness of Lexington. But neither a real avenue, by the highest standards.

Mungo was probably lying with his wife at this very minute enjoying a Sunday cuddle. "Where do you suppose that uptight bastard is right now—off some place polishing his prose?" "Who? Oh, you mean Max. He isn't so bad." "Yeah, miserable tight-ass creep. Chopping up some beautiful actress he doesn't deserve, with his little mincing shears. Take that (squeak), you dreadful little creature, and that." "Oh, Gene, you know that isn't fair." "Yeah, well maybe. But tell me, does he ever just enjoy himself? Does he ever unzip that gray little mind and give it some air? Does he ever . . ." She smothers his mouth with a hot kiss. They drift off. Jamison is forgotten.

Next scene. "Tell us about nature, Uncle Gene. Tell us about wild flowers and the trail of the bluebonnet." Justin's eyes all alight now, the puffy languor gone. No talk of hotdogs or soda, but a child's wonderful curiosity. Max trudged along. Gene had taken the child on his knee and was making marvelous patterns with his hands. The child-mind awakening . . .

I've got to change, I've got to change. Even if it means becoming a teeny bit more like Mungo. He returned home and shaved. No one really gave a shit whether he returned home or not, whether he shaved or not. That was the beautiful thing about freedom.

The critics' circle was in session when he arrived. They met in the Asshole Room of the Hotel Asshole, as far as Max was concerned. His mind tasted quite foul now, and spewed little bits of garbage into his mouth. He had better not talk too much tonight. He had not written his review, and he felt guilty and hungover about that; not, as he had hoped, roguish and liberated. They sat at a long baize-covered table with various-colored potions in front of them, looking, to Max's yellow eye, like wizards, alchemists, dwarfs.

They were talking, his fatheaded circle, about the admission of new members. Jack Flashman, wise guy emeritus at the other news magazine, was on the agenda. "Frankly," said Isabel Nutley of *Women's Thoughts*, "I don't think he quite comes up to our standards." "If we had any standards at all, half of you wouldn't be here," growled the tireless Bruffin. "Gentlemen, gentlemen," said the chairman. "I don't know—who writes the stuff on that magazine anyway? How can you tell? Flashman may be dead, for all we know." "He's a gossip writer, for Christsake. What does he know about the theater?" "What do any of you know about the theater?" "Gentlemen, gentlemen." "Frankly, if Flashman gets in, I quit. I can't stand the guy." "That's too damn bad, we'll miss you, honey, but Flashman happens to write for a very important magazine. You can't just ignore it." "What's wrong with gossip writing? Most of you don't even reach *that* level." "Gentlemen."

As he looked at their small maniac faces round the table, fighting like cannibals over a dead missionary's pants, Max thought, What you need around here is nothing less than a spiritual rebirth. Let me bring it to you! Let me start the ball rolling. But their eyes were crazed, myopic, their voices high and fanatical; they operated out of little glass bowls, and no one could come in.

"What do you say, Max?"

"I say, why not?" Max said with staring eyes. "Why should any man carry through life the stain of being rejected by this damn fool society?"

"Well, that's true," conceded Bruffin.

Let's hear it now for spiritual rebirth. You too,

Bruffin! Down on your knees, you dog. Can't you see that we *all* have to change? I'm not the only one. You're all self-important asses. Or threadbare clowns. Or pretentious hacks. No exceptions, right? You all know that about each other, at least. Take a vote. The room was rimy with contempt; he had never seen such mutual loathing in any group.

So let me lead you into the waters of salvation. My tattered little scout troop, my bee-keepers, my bank clerks. Good enough critics, at least, to know each other's worthlessness. Let us begin with that. Lord, they are not much, I know. But take them for what they are. What's that you say, Lord? You'll call us? I see. Yes, I quite understand.

These meetings always gave Max a sovereign headache. All that trade talk. He couldn't connect with it at all tonight. There were too many serious thoughts to be shuffled solemnly around his own showroom. Did these other critics have lives too? He supposed so. Cold sweats. Silent screaming in the night. Isabel Nutley crouched in a corner of her bathtub watching the water rise. Each must come in here sometimes clamoring for rebirth and deploring the triviality of the others; they probably took turns at it. Tonight was old Max's turn. Nothing important.

"I guess I have to vote against Flashman," he said, reversing himself on Bruffin, "if there's any point to having these meetings at all. He's the kind of guy who'll vote for Jayne Mansfield as actress of the year. A cut-up."

"I'm for him," said Bruffin, swirling his 7-Up. "He writes cleaner prose than anyone in this room. He's also a *complete* sell-out, unlike the rest of you, which gives him a certain kind of integrity. And, above all, he is an *artist* in gossip . . ."

Blood swam across Max's eyes. "Harold, let's make it brief. You give me a pain in the ass."

Bruffin waved a hand. "Is that so? You should take something for it."

"Yes, I think I will." Max stood up awkwardly. He hadn't hit anyone in years and was uncertain of the actual motion of the arm. Was it like a swimming stroke or more like casting a fly? He hadn't done much of those either. Movie punches, stage punches—it would come to him.

Bruffin did not rise to meet him, but sat smirking; as if a punch from Max would be a marvelous giveaway. What did I tell you—hysteria, panic. All these sell-outs are alike. Next he'll be setting fire to the curtains. It gave Max a moment's pause. The obvious way out was verbal. "The trouble with people like you, Bruffin, is that they don't fight when someone calls them a pain in the ass." Not bad, but not good enough. The blood circling his scalp would not settle for that. This was the one spiritual solution he hadn't thought of last night and he was not going to talk himself out of it. He picked up Bruffin by the lapel and removed his glasses as delicately as a dentist, hoping now that Bruffin would hold the smirk just a moment longer; and wheeled his arm round somehow until his knuckles rattled against Bruffin's teeth. Surprisingly hard teeth. A squish of blood traced over his fingers. My God, that felt good. Isabel Nutley screamed pleasantly and rushed for him. Several writhing critics pinned him: it must be a pleasure for them to move their bodies for a change, to be firm with someone. He let them. He had no intention of socking Bruffin again.

The latter had put his hand to his mouth and down again, and it seemed now to contain a tooth. How about that? I knocked a tooth out. Bruffin suddenly darted forward, whimpering like a small animal, and hit Max a soft blow on the eye like a girl. Great! No more talk about hysteria now. Hitting a man when his arms are pinned, indeed. Bruffin was led away still whimpering and staring at his tooth.

Max scooped up his coat and left without speaking to anybody. That seemed best. There was a sense of shock among the critics, which would give way to downright joy as the physical threat receded and they resumed their lives as voyeurs. Critics should do this to each other more often. Magnificent if they fell to clubbing each other right now.

He felt elated all the way home, until with his head down over his shoes, he thought, My God, what was that all about? His new spiritual solution: the gods had made him mad. O.K., O.K., don't take it too hard. Just blowing off steam; lots of good, sane people do that. Bankers and such. And God, did Bruffin ever lose face, crying like a baby over his tooth. But a racking remorse kept Max's neck bent until he could barely raise it. Loss of control was not what he had expected when he started his spiritual odyssey last night.

18

Max's immediate boss at *Now*, Harvey Salter, tsar of the back of the book, was part of the new wave of *Now* people. If you said to him, as Max had at their first interview, that you thought the magazine was vulgar and superficial, he would scratch his stubby nose and say, "Yes. We're trying to correct that." If you singled out some particular item you especially disliked, Salter would remember it gloomily and say that he hadn't much cared for it either. Given enough time and pressure, he would give up on the whole magazine for you.

Salter was the man who had started hiring people like Max in the first place, and he watched over his eggheads carefully. He lunched with them from time to time, in the bleak executive dining room, and there was talk over the Bloody Marys about the crumby state of the theater. And sometimes at the theater itself, Max would feel Salter breathing gently on his neck from the row in back. Salter never commented on Max's work, but he kept him on edge with this damn intelligent interest of his.

In fact, he spooked Max quite a piece. Harvey had gone to *Now* as a junior seminarian and had been there ever since, no matter how distastefully he appeared to view it; he had survived purges large and small and had moved up steadily under a variety of regimes, getting glummer and more sneaky-diffident as he went. Until now he sat above the world in immaculate white shirt sleeves, and looking like a man who lived on indigestion pills, although no one had ever seen him take one.

Max knew in his bones that if one went to see Salter and told him that one was suffering a crisis of the spirit, he would understand perfectly ("Oh God, yes—I have those myself"), and charter a plane to Tibet for you. Now, Inc. was a formidably kindly organization and they were always sending employees off on six months' leaves. So what if the employees usually came back three months early in a muck sweat? It wasn't the magazine's fault that no one could trust such kindness.

Max made an appointment to see Salter on Monday, and then cancelled it. He imagined the scene afterwards in the power suite. "Jamison's beginning to crack. Good. Send him away for a while. They're always weaker and softer when they get back. They're *ours* then." A synchronized shifting of cigars. "They can't work anywhere else after a company vacation. You can do what you like with them. Put 'em in Religion, put

169

'em in Finance. They'll go without a sound." A mighty rustle of trouser legs. "They've admitted weakness, you see. And that's the name of the game, isn't it?" A great growl of assent.

Jamison didn't trust any of them a damn inch. He didn't understand people like that. He had never worked for the power crowd before, and all he had to go on was fantasy. Salter was the company spy, the understanding chap in the bar who talked you into blurting things. He really loved *Now*, old Salter, would lie and cheat and steal for it. But when he fell, in the inevitable men's-room fight, his skull would split open and reveal a small radio.

Max typed a quick, bad review in his old style and, loathing himself more than ever, handed it in sourly. He went to lunch with his hands shaking, the way old *Now* hands did. It suddenly seemed tremendously important not to show his weakness; and as he looked along the bar, he saw that that was the motive of all of them.

Jack Flashman cruised up. What was he doing over here? This wasn't his bar. He must have sniffed carrion. Flashman had certainly never had a spiritual crisis himself, but he probably enjoyed them in others. Must not show weakness in front of Flashman. "Hi Max, how goes?" Notice the probing question, the sly, gross man behind it. Ah crap, Flashman meant no harm.

"I hear you threw a punch at Bruffin last night."

So that's what he was doing here. Checking out a rumor. "Who told you that?"

"I have those meetings bugged, didn't you know? I know whose standards I come up to and whose I don't."

"You do, huh? You wouldn't care to name your leak,

170

would you? Our humble meetings are supposed to be confidential."

"Isabel Nutley talks in her sleep. So what did you slug Bruffin for? In your very own words?"

"Don't you know? Or are you trying to spring a second leak?"

"Just double-checking. What I heard was that Bruffin wanted me in the group, and you called him an obscenity and hit him. Is that right?"

It was hard to tell under the stiff clown's face and the shrill bantering voice; but it appeared that Flashman was genuinely angry. Oh great, that's just what I need this morning. A new enemy.

"Your informant is a troublemaker, Jack. Probably Bruffin himself, trying to suck up to you. Did he say I pulled a knife on him?"

Flashman shook his head. "It wasn't Bruffin."

"Well, whoever it was, let me send this message back. Anyone who violates confidence like that is inherently untrustworthy. You buy that?"

Flashman was definitely trying to glower. A grand enemy to find in your In-tray on a Monday morning, a dealer in theatrical gossip who could spread the tale from coast to coast in a matter of hours; or, if his own magazine didn't go for it, could trade it to some dirtier journal and get Max that way.

Max had never imagined worrying about a thing like this. He was not a public figure; his backbiting covered a small area—parts of Manhattan, some houses in Connecticut. He had never realized the jolt to the nerves that went with big-time gossip.

He suddenly found himself almost pleading with

171

Flashman. "For Godsake, Jack—that's the most distorted account I've ever heard of anything. O.K. I voted you down, that's true. But only because I don't think you belong in that particular group. And believe me, that's no insult."

"Nice going, Max babes. Very nice footwork. You voted me down to spare me the pain of not 'belonging.' Of being the only black kid on the block. I appreciate that."

"Listen, it's just a pretentious little group of would-be highbrows, half of whom are certifiably insane . . ."

"In other words, serious critics. Unlike me. Don't go on, Max. I'm very quick. Just tell me about the fight."

"I don't know. It just happened. Harold was being snotty. He called you a—never mind." Max hadn't meant to curry favor with Flashman by tattling. This was awful. "I just blew up and hit him. One punch. You're not going to print that, are you?"

Flashman blinked in back of his bifocals. "Print it? Where? Who wants to read about a nothing fight between two unknown critics? Who ever heard of Bruffin outside of Manhattan? Who ever heard of you outside your office?"

Oh God. To beg for mercy and be told that you didn't need it. The ruthless power of the press would spare him after all.

"You eating, or just drinking?" said Flashman.

"Just drinking, it begins to look like."

Flashman's face suddenly slumped, in a surprising gesture. "You know, Max, this is ridiculous, but I'd like to get into that damn society of yours. It would help me at my shop. They have very twisted ideas over there.

Also, it would help my confidence, which is not too hot right now."

"*Your* confidence? You're kidding."

"Right. I've been striking out with too many broads lately. Those scores tell you how you're doing. Naming my magazine gets me halfway to bed, at least with the kind of chicks I want to get to bed with. But then I get stuck. They must sense something—job insecurity, identity crisis."

"How's the wife and kids, Jack?"

"They're O.K. So listen, will you put in a word for me at your next outing? I'd appreciate it."

Oh, sure. Why not? "You can have my place if you like, Jack. I only go twice a year, to pick up my gossip." The triviality was suddenly suffocating. What Flashman obviously needed was rebirth, nothing less would do. Maybe we could found a monastery or something together.

"You can afford to be arrogant, Max. I can't." Flashman the Flip having his noonday drinky-poos. Which was better—a vice-like grope, or a voice-like gripe?

"I'm glad you think so. I'd been thinking of giving it up. But you encourage me to persevere."

Max decided to go straight home after lunch. He couldn't face the visual assault of a screening, or the strain of trying to disentangle the sounds. Perhaps he should lie down and recite "God is love" until he fell into a deep, untroubled sleep. Or ring a small bell to summon the monks to prayer.

You know the trouble, Max? No, tell me what the trouble is. All right, I will. You're like the old alcoholic who's too intelligent for AA. You go to the meetings with the best intentions, and you listen to those wind-bags baring their souls and unwinding their bandages and finding new strength; and you just can't do it. The wise man, the holy man, says, Look, suppose the only road to health lies that way, through stupidity and bad taste? Can't you take a few steps? And your palms sweat, you're scared out of your mind, but no, you can't do it. You leave the meeting and walk back into hell.

As Max wandered home, he imagined a red-light district lined with Christian Science reading rooms, Zen institutes, Scientology labs, faith healers, a gaudy, sleazy gin lane that the Pilgrim must fight his way through. But when he got home, there were no trumpets sounding for him, only a buzzing refrigerator. He pulled the blind and lay down. Go on now, say it. "Love, love, love." "Hara Krishna." Anything. His mouth twisted like a persimmon. I can't do that crap.

The phone rang. This is it! The game is up. He reached out a manicured hand. Why would a man like me care about his nails? Why the twelve suits? Please, some other time perhaps. No more questions today. This here on the phone was Miss Weaver, Mr. Salter's secretary. Having now obtained Mr. Jamison, she must proceed to obtain Mr. Salter. This was a lengthy business, it involved dredging men's rooms and other possible hiding places, and finally a thrilling chase across roofs. That was how long it took for Harvey Salter to answer his own calls.

Max, woozy from Bloody Marys, went through the normal death spasms while waiting. Salter had obviously read Max's latest copy, had seen at once that Max was having a spiritual crisis, and had already made the arrangements to have him spirited out of the country. Two weeks with the Dalai Lama and we'll have you back on your feet. "Max, is that you, Max?"

"Yes, hello there, Harvey."

"Well, Max, how about lunch tomorrow? I'd like to talk to you."

Tomorrow? I'll be dead tomorrow. "Is it something about the column I handed in? I can do it over this afternoon if you like."

"Column? No, I haven't seen that yet. I'm sure it's fine. All your work is fine."

Oh. Not the column. What a joke on me. Worrying about the column and all that. Max had always despised anxiety cases. But now, as he struggled for rebirth and transcendence, he found the smalls of life getting to him worse than ever. What did he care about his column? Being fired from *Now* would cover him with glory in his old set; his marshal's baton would be restored to him and his old place at the mess. Capital to have you back, Jamison. Yet here he was, writhing along the floor, offering to rewrite when no rewrite was called for. The way of the Pilgrim had strange beginnings.

"Lunch, yes, fine. Doesn't conflict with the old schedule, not one whit." Aye-yie-yie. He put the phone down, took off his pants and folded them neatly and got into bed and slept freakishly through the rest of the afternoon and night, randomly exhausted and desolate.

Lunch with Harvey Salter was like Greco-Roman wrestling. It was possible that he was actually quite guileless, but Max couldn't take the chance. Max prepared himself with aftershave lotion and a vicious

175

squirt of deodorant and wondered whether he was turning into a fag. Perhaps that was his problem all along. It
would certainly break the log jam to find out.

He kicked it around in the taxi on the way to lunch
and found it didn't interest him much. Even if some
smooth lawyer could talk him into believing it, it
wouldn't make any important difference. It wasn't the
big breakthrough. Now, tell me that I'm not a *critic,*
and I'll listen. Tell me that criticism is a social evil, for
which nuns were once flogged and burned, and you'll
have my attention. But homosexuality—I don't know,
I'm too old to care. Burning incense, picking up sailors,
doing exercises for the waistline. All that. Max knew
from bitter Broadway experience that he was really a
fag deep down, but it would take years to dig his fag-
dom up and make it operational, by which time he
would be too old to hobble along the waterfront every
night.

For once they were not having lunch in the power
dining room of the *Now* building. Salter had picked, of
all spots, the Harvard Club. Was this a clue? Harvey
seemed nervous and gloomy. This was certainly a clue.
They dragged themselves through the wastes of brown
leather, and moldering old grads; but then Salter
changed his mind and said, "Let's have a drink out
here." He ordered a double martini, hardly the drink for
a man in a position of responsibility.

Salter sat in ominous silence, making spidery baskets
with his fingers. He looked as if he was going to ask if
Max had had a good trip downtown. The blow might
not fall until dessert. Max couldn't wait that long.

"Did you get to read the column yet?"

"Oh yes, yes."

"What did you think? Was it O.K.?"

"I thought it was quite perceptive. We're very pleased with you at *Now*."

Back into the slick womb of his stuffed armchair. I don't know if I can take much more of this. I have not been reborn yet, so what has happened to my pride? The minister, a big black man in a surplice, had just taken away his clothes for the baptism, and gone off laughing. There's no water around here, boy. Salter sat opposite, glooming.

"Tell me," he said at last. "I hear you've left your wife, Max."

"Yes, yes. I have."

Salter nodded. So that was it. Max had flunked the morals test. *Now* had its code. You can't serve in the Court of St. James's with your fly undone, dash it all.

Salter sighed. "I wish I had the courage to do that."

"What? What courage?"

"You know what I mean. Telling her, telling the children." Telling the board of directors? "God, it's awful. Here I am, forty-eight. Dying slowly. Nothing will happen if it doesn't happen soon."

"What's the matter with your marriage?"

"Nothing, really." Salter opened his basket and closed it again quickly. "It's just awful. All this is in strictest confidence, you understand."

"Of course."

"I had to talk to somebody, and when I heard what you'd done, I thought, why not you? Besides, I thought you'd know what I meant by 'awful.'"

"Yes, that's true." Become just a little broken and

177

everyone comes to you for spiritual help. The glass in your eye shatters and they think you have healing powers.

"It's like going home to a hospital every day. Emily moves around very quietly, like a nurse, arranging the flowers. I have a drink and lie down. I'm dying."

"How old are the kids?"

"Nine, fourteen, and eighteen. Pete is in college."

"Can't you wait a little longer?"

"I don't know. I fix things in the basement, and make fires—you know, to pass the time. But the days are absolutely endless. By three o'clock on a Saturday I'm at my wit's end."

"What about your work?"

"Yes, work, religion, sports. I've used work for a long time, for more than it's worth. A man needs something else, I need hardly tell you."

"Is there another girl?"

"Oh Lord, no. It's a nice idea, but it's not what I'm talking about. I mean something like joy in the house. My kids are so listless. Emily gets up quietly every morning and goes down to the kitchen—do you know what I mean?—getting out the corn flakes and things. She's an excellent woman."

You and your quiet desperation. No more Chekhov for you for at least six months.

"I hate to bring it up, Harvey, but does her excellence include, you know?"

"Definitely."

Salter looked as if he'd missed his last bus. His problem was so simple. It was being forty-eight. And nothing would cure it. Rebirth for you too, sir. Join the bandwagon, roll down to the Holy River.

"Well, God knows," said Max, "I wouldn't presume to give advice to anyone right now, about anything. But I would say, hang in there if you possibly can."

"You would, eh?" Not the most sparkling advice ever heard.

"God, yes. You have no idea how you'll miss your kids. How anxious you'll feel all the time. There isn't a woman in the world who can keep your mind off that."

O sage, O giver of wisdom.

"Trapped, huh? In a post-Christian but pre-modern soul."

No wonder Salter had risen in *Now*, with his sure grasp of Western thought. "Having children is one of the two or three useful things I've done," said Max. "No, it isn't even that. I love my son *unambiguously*. I would die for him. It's the only nice simple thought I've ever had."

Good boy, Max. Die for him—by George, sir. It brings tears. Yet Max meant it and was glad to have said it. Not that it did anything for Salter's gloom. "Trapped," he repeated, and after that they talked about other things, and Salter spoke with lively interest about the theater and world affairs as if he was the happiest little editor in God's green world.

19

Helen had left town as promised, for a place up the Hudson called Windemere. Max supposed he should have tried to get a restraining order or something. But bringing them back in leg irons was hardly the way to win hearts. Or he could go up to their new place and park morosely outside, driving them all slowly mad. The trouble was, he didn't want to tear the children in two, and he didn't want them to think he'd given up without a struggle. There seemed nothing in between.

He did phone a lawyer he knew, but it didn't help much. Whatever he decided to do would take time and run into money, the lawyer explained. He asked one or two divorced friends what they would do and found that their situations had differed from his in certain crucial aspects. Anyway, asking for advice always made him feel like a small man with bad teeth, so he didn't pursue these inquiries.

The next Saturday, he rented a car and drove up to Windemere, just to see what it was like up there. It was much colder than the city, on a barren, smoky spring day. Max sat in the Plymouth, by the side of the main road, thinking that this might be a good place to start his monastery. He pictured blue-faced monks, shaking with the cold, trudging serenely up the rise ahead of him: Bruffin and Salter and Flashman, lashed together by vast rosary beads. Jamison leading them on with head bowed, the saintliest of them all, kind but firm, holy but oh so human, a critic in the fields of the Lord.

I hate to say it, but you were born in the wrong century, Abbot Jamison. Great fat scholar, mysteriously dapper, at the head of the friars' table, that's more like it. It is rumored that Abbot Jamison levitates and plays chess with the devil. For the souls of his charges. Won a stained-glass window just the other night. But his annotated version of Bede is perhaps his sturdiest achievement. Pungent marginalia, years ahead of their time. Dirty but perceptive. "Four Stars"—*Anglo-Saxon Chronicle*.

Max really hoped that this free association would jerk something loose: that behind the ready-made phrases, strung like bracelets, there lurked something looser and more fluid. He did not believe in a real Self buried since childhood (you can't bury something that deep and expect it to live), but in some kind of unformed substance from which a new self might be fashioned. Didn't know whether he believed that either, but he couldn't think of anything better to believe. If he went crazy in the process, perhaps it was for the best.

Meanwhile, he had to decide something about Helen and the kids.

Possible scene 1: Justin suddenly materializing down the road on wobbling bike. "Daddy! What are you doing here?" "Well, I'm just sitting and thinking, as a matter of fact." "What are you doing that for?—Hey, gang, I think Daddy's going crazy. That's what's happening to your whole generation, isn't it, Dad?" "You're not Justin at all. Stop that! Put me down at once!" No, seriously, he didn't want them finding him here. He couldn't face any kind of embarrassment.

Scene 2: Stalking into the house, old-fashioned style. "I want to see the boys." "They're out bird-watching with Gene." Or "They're in the toolshed and they don't want to see you." "I *demand* to see my boys, Helen!" or "I'll wait" or "You can't do this to me." "Oh, can't I?" or "Bite him, Rover." Justin's voice: "Tell him to go away." Charles: "Who is that man?"

He bent across the steering wheel. His head felt heavy enough to drown a man. It had been a terrible week. He had written an apology to Bruffin on Tuesday and received a stiff, ungenerous response on Thursday, questioning his sanity. Don't people know when it's not the time to question one's sanity? He had asked Flashman to have a drink with him after the theater Thursday night and been turned down cold. He had failed Flashman in *his* moth-eaten crisis and was not going to be given a second chance. Then Max had phoned those divorced friends and sensed, in place of wise sympathy, nothing but lubricious curiosity. He had written a terrible review for *Rearview*.

What would Lord Chesterfield have done about it?

"Dear Justin, try to look at it my way, sir. You will find that being a grown-up is not so damn easy. To be honorable in your profession is something. You're not impressed with that? Well, perhaps you're right not to be. I remember despising *my* father too. For exactly opposite reasons to yours. Maybe that's what we're supposed to do and William Inge's mouthings are correct. It's a little damn hard, though.

"All right, forget about that. What about you? Do you think you can be a better man than I? It isn't that easy, my boy. Even being mediocre isn't that easy. And I believe I'm a little better than mediocre. Well, I don't want to keep coming back to me. Just think of me as someone who wishes you well. My own parents were very good in that way, spoiled me, made me feel like a little king or godlet. But I despised them anyway. So you can't win, can you?

"Any damn fool can be a grown-up, I used to think. Ha—just let me up on that high wire! But I don't know too many people who've made it. You should see my friends. If they make it at work, they lose it at home. Make it at home, lose it at work. Christ. Sometimes you lose at both. To make it with one child would be worth it, but one can't demand that, can one?"

His invisible letter wasn't making any sense. He couldn't say any of these things to Justin for another fifteen years at least. He is just a small boy, don't take him so seriously. Raise him as some old arrowsmith would, teaching him to bend the bow and to talk gently to women. Not to make fun of things. To have some God to repair to when things get ugly. That's all that's required for now.

I don't want to force myself on him. And yet that is the way to teach. By prying the jaws open and forcing myself in. Like a lion tamer.

Max was none too sure how to get to Helen's house, so he drove into what passed for a town center. The gas station was really a grocery store that sold old newspapers. Or so it seemed at first glance. A fat lady, obviously deaf, presided over this mélange.

"Can you tell me—"

"You don't have to shout, I'm not deaf."

"I'm sorry. Can you tell me how to get to St. Edmund's Lane?"

This involved sending for her nephew who was doing something nameless out back. An unnaturally tall boy in a wool shirt. Clearly would have a speech defect of some kind. Possibly a harelip. His people had salted him away up here out of very shame.

Wrong again. He turned out to be one of those masterful young snots studying for a Ph.D. in map reading. Max went back to the car primed with most delicate, nuanced instructions. He noted again that the spiritual life seemed to be full of hostility; one heard of the great saints flying into arrogant rages. After every bout of remorse and self-examination, Max had wanted to hit someone. He could see some vile quality in every stranger, some grotesque character flaw sticking out like a growth. Cover yourself, sir. (His own character flaw was a hairy mole tastefully concealed in the armpit.)

He drove on in a lather of hatred for humanity as such.

Helen's new house was a bungalow deep in weeds. There was no movement about it, so he assumed they were all out gaffing salmon or gathering spore. Little Sir Egghead—no, he had been interested in those things himself once upon a time. He had bird-nested with the best of them, had classified mushrooms and scoured the country in his rainboots. He was a born indexer. When his collections were scattered by some moving men, he lost interest in nature.

Then what happened, Mr. Jamison? I'm glad you asked that, honey. I discovered that critical method, rigorous intelligence was a great way to get girls in the sack. So I limited my collecting to that. Max felt his own sex begin to gurgle, as his phantom interviewer, a kid from Wellesley, started to disrobe in a fever of investigative curiosity. Actually, Max had started collecting his psychic belongings long before women had anything to do with it; his boyhood was an exercise in empire building.

Battle of Parsley School playground, turning point. He remembered a wire fence, like a prison compound. A concrete floor. Baskets limp as kitchen mops. A boy with a small face whinnying, "Max is an A.K. Max is a teacher's pet." Max was new to this kind of attack. His first two years of school had been spent mostly at home. Brief case of asthma, long since cleared up. No complications. Delicate case of spoiling by parent, according to Helen. Why was this boy shouting at him then? Not clear. Well anyway, clout him for now. Max went over to the jibbering Italian boy (Nicholas Pietrozini from South Boston) and pasted him—nose, mouth, and chin.

Sensation. Pietrozini hadn't meant anything like that, it was just second-degree kidding. The crowd fell back in burbling awe. In sheer ignorance of school protocol, Max had managed to make the world safe for Jamison. For good measure, Pietrozini's head clanged richly against the concrete wall of the handball court and he passed out cold. Any damn fool can be prince regent in his own home; but Max was free to show off at school, too.

He became the class grind and nobody minded. He felt at times like a distinguished foreign visitor, delegate from the Kingdom of Mind. Who was he showing off to, exactly? To his teachers? Those mediocrities? Perhaps. To show them who was master. To his hearty mother and pale, clever father? Better. His father was, in a sense, his first editor, and editors must be dominated. Max hit the books with a kind of muscular energy that baffled and even frightened many people. And he liked them to hear his brain throbbing, sense the power of it.

Not exactly the education of a Heart—yet Max had one advantage in that world too. He was almost completely free from envy. Once the other person, whoever it was, had signaled "Goodness, you're smart" and little Max had had a chance to contemplate the moment, like God gazing upon himself, he was capable of uninterrupted fairness. (This, he understood, still made him close to unique in New York.) He had several friends in those days dumber than himself and he never primped in front of them. Sam Goldpaper had praised him for a smart goy, the only one he had ever met. Jack Davis, thick-necked mechanic, talked cars with him, demonstrating how to strip a car, and Max, aged twelve now, had listened politely and let Davis be king. Max was good at his specialty, and he respected people who were good at theirs. Of course, his specialty was more important; much more important; infinitely more important (his point of view at thirteen, nineteen, twenty-five respectively), but he preferred a good mechanic to a bad poet, from the first.

Does intellect cut you off from other people? Is thinking unnatural? What says the Pope on this point?

Sports, sir. Pius XII plumped for bicycle racing; others prefer a manly game of golf. Get those poisons of doubt moving, chase them around the system, out of the little opening at the bottom. Max had hated sports from the beginning, individually and exhaustively. Could never really admire a Pope who was hung up on them. Football: having your brains jarred by someone who had none to lose himself. Bounced off the frosty ground by Minotaurs. Knees in the face. And penalized every time he tried to get even. Baseball: boredom punctuated by humiliation. Basketball: what could one say of basketball? Why should a man surrender his weapon, his brain, and enter these uncontrolled competitions? Max was big for his age and could lumber along formidably, but this had limited use in most games, and he gave it all up as soon as the authorities would allow. Nowadays, he occasionally skied, walked, swam—solitary forms of movement that kept the stomach flat and ready for bed.

In the army, he had vaguely supposed he would have to hit someone again to establish his right to privacy. But his years of immunity had put confidence in his face: some look of violence or brutality about him, a dreamy arrogance. The dummies rather took to him, because this kind of look is good luck. Although there was no question of keeping in contact with him later. He was a neat man who had no trouble with drill sergeants. He did have a set-to with the chaplain, who tried to press him into observance. They argued about Frazer's *Golden Bough* and the authenticity of the gospels, and the chaplain gave him up as a waste of time.

Smart chaplain. Rev. Tomkins must have sensed that even if he had won the argument, he would not have picked up a soul. Because Max was basically irreligious. Church struck no sparks with him at all. His father practiced it with an air of "I have to, but don't you bother." Max had looked into the matter solemnly in college, had had it out with the Catholics, went to services where he stood blankly and left, with the certainty that he was religion-proof. Except for occasional blasphemous purposes. At that time he still thought it a virtue to discard ideas, not knowing that winter was coming.

So—no sport, no religion. Unnatural boy. We don't even have to bother the Pope with this. It can be handled on a lower level. This unnatural boy has made a God of himself. Very well. You know what theology says about that. We'll leave him to his own devices. Let him be God as long as he likes. All by himself. He will of course go mad, pluck out his eyes, skin and boil himself, feather and tar, roast and baste—well, you know what they do. Look it up in Dante. Next case, please.

It was getting late. Still nobody home. Max decided to leave in five minutes, then sank back into reverie.

Max saw himself kneeling in full episcopal robes. In some movie house. This is my church, your worship. I have not made a God of myself but, if anything, of this. Of art. Oh, have you really? Yes, sir. Well, let's look up your record on that.

First interested in drawing and music, usual business. Hum-de-hum. The inquisitor's glasses kept slipping, in order to confuse Max. He also kept shifting from ferocious madman to absent-minded civil servant, as the occasion warranted. At moments he could have passed for Cary Grant. "Here we are. Poetry." Undoes the ribbon around a violet folder. "Too snotty for Longfellow, I see. From the very beginning. Can you explain that, sir?" "Simple good taste." "I see. Simple good taste. *Do you really believe that?* Are you aware, sir, that many fine judges have discovered unexpected merit in Mr. Longfellow?" "I can't help that." "Has it occurred to you, moreover, that a small boy should start by liking Longfellow, whatever he may decide later? That not to argues a paralyzing affectation, a deep-rooted desire to show off, at the expense of art and honest feeling? Have you ever done anything else really, except use art to thrust yourself forward, as a fashionable priest uses religion? This is your church, quite right—but there's nobody in it but you." "You understand this is quite unfair. You sound like a French Catholic novel." "Whatever you say, Max. You're the one who invented me, you know."

May God, if there is a God, be kinder to me than I am to myself. He fidgeted, unthinking, with the ignition. The self-congratulation of former years had gone rancid, and he could find no decent place for his mind to rest. His sexuality was a coarse, grunting nightmare. His good taste was based on calculations of self-interest, which had become second nature. He no longer had to tell himself not to like Longfellow, his lightning calculator took care of it. His machine worked so smoothly that it even told him when it was all right to start liking Longfellow again. Rearrange the above materials and you've almost got it. "When I was young, it was fashionable to dismiss Longfellow. But now that one rereads him . . ."

Hah. Why aren't you thinking about your son? You came up here to find him, didn't you? To fling yourself through the door in humble appeal. "Helen, I want the boy." "Why, Max. Something has happened to you. You're different, more human." "Suffering is what does it, my dear. Suffering and humiliation and, oh you know." Stumbling blindly, winsomely forward. Lemon rind now around his teeth, he was smiling viciously at his own invention.

"I cannot change, I cannot make myself change," he said slowly and stiffly. He couldn't see the children in this state. He had flogged himself half to death, and he hadn't changed a bit.

The cars plunged at him with murderous yellow eyes. Max hadn't driven for a year, and had forgotten what they were up to out here, maiming, killing, terrorizing each other. Another excellent way to lose yourself that had completely slipped his mind. He gunned his own motor with heavy, godlike foot. A touch on the wheel now and he could take a family of six to blazing destruction. Children with bandaged heads, father neatly impaled on steering wheel, woman screaming, howling Max's name into the night. Like a coyote. He slowed down again, with palms wet and foot trembling.

Max stopped at a plastic palace off the highway for a hamburger, didn't notice the waitress and kept calling the wrong ones over. *This* isn't a real scene, he thought, only a piece of punctuation. Meals under $3.95 are not real. Every waitress had the same puffy face and sunken gray eyes and badly hung skirt. They must have another one out back. This was intolerable. He left in a rage.

Back safe in the car, he tried to turn his leaking free association on someone else's troubles. Every fool knew that that was the sneaky way of the Pilgrim. Compassion. Use the other guy. Harvey Salter and his dying marriage must have been sent to him for a reason. He pictured Salter now, against a dark sky, mowing the lawn by candlelight or fixing the den. Hammering, trying unconsciously to hit his finger and draw the pain away from his head. Salter's unhappiness may be my greatest ally, thought Max, distracting him from his otherwise total absorption in my case. But then he might want to create a diversion by firing me. Plant the pain in some neutral rectum. Look, who are we talking about, you or Salter? Get on with the story. Let's have Emily Salter come shuffling into the game room at some point carrying a flowerpot. Her face is puffy and her eyes sunken. The lights go up and there is brief applause for the set.

EMILY: Where should I put this, dear?

HARVEY: How the Christ should I know where to put

it? You might try up your keester. (*Remorse-stricken*) Oh God, I didn't mean that. Put it on the pool table, why don't you. It'll be a great centerpiece.

EMILY: You don't mean that, do you, dear? I've made another mistake, haven't I? (*Wanders out carrying flowerpot, her controlling metaphor, crying softly. Harvey emits low wail, starts methodically hammering thumb.*)

Max was sick of his story, almost physically sick. His goddamned second-rate imagination, neither funny nor true, panted doggedly up the stairs anyway and followed the Salters into the bedroom. They are lying side by side, modestly exhausted after making love for (check the meter) the 5,000th time. A *Now* milestone. Absolutely nothing is wrong. Harvey has noticed a burst vein on his belly that wasn't there before but you don't call the papers about that.

Emily is one of those people who live outside of New York. Her eye is slow, her tongue heavy. She has the reflexes of a three-toed sloth. "Happy?" she whispers. Harvey nods sullenly. A burst vein is nothing to carry on about. The traffic is condensing outside New York, and all motion on the highway has ceased, temporarily. Max sits in his shiny bower of tin, trying to turn his imagination off. If he ever succeeds, he will never turn it on again, he swears.

Harvey moves closer to his wife on the vast Louis XVI four-poster and whispers: "I'm worried about Max."

"So am I," she whispers back.

"I think about him constantly."

"So do I," she avers. "What else is there to think about, when you come down to it?"

They moan and cling to each other. "Isn't it awful about Max?" they agree.

Back in New York, he returned the car with a show of credit cards. The girl smiled at him, and he thought of asking her out, but in a minute he had forgotten her completely. Returning a car wasn't real. Or if it was, it shouldn't be. Your children were real. They could be proved. The rest was farce.

Burns Mantle's *Best Plays of 1923-4*. George Jean Nathan. Little man made of glass. Not so bad. John Mason Brown. Tweed. Brooks Atkinson. Wet tweed. He ran his finger accusingly along the new book shelf. His colleagues. Good God. He selected a picture book, *Fifty Years of Unforgettable Theatre*, opened it, stared at the set pieces. Seven heads including the maid turn to the French window: where chalk-faced, radiant Gertrude Lawrence stands framed. Eight heads including butler and maid turn to Clifton Webb gesturing like a dummy in an Abercrombie & Fitch display at a man in a wheelchair. Even the active characters are waxworks. Moments that will live. Out of camera range sit the immortalizers, Brooks and Percy and Alex, with cheeks rouged and straw peeping from their dress shirts. "Brought glamour back to Broadway, joy to this tired old heart. Hilarious, radiant. Miss Merman will take no nonsense from a song. The Lunts, ah what can one say of the Lunts? Miss Cornell honored, let's say it, ennobled us, with her presence." And the waxy faces beam back stiffly; even the little maid in the long gray dress at the end of the line who will grow up to be—Sophie Warbuck—and stand in the French windows herself someday, holding her arms up, giddy with ego and happiness, half mad, convinced that Burns Mantle matters. Yes—Burns Mantle!

He snapped the book shut. Thinking about his profession was almost as bad as thinking about his chil-dren.

20

Aquarius in Taurus and vice versa. The sea turned to wood and bonfires were lit at the globe's corners to warn the fish. That at least was the way it appeared to him. "Got to make it up with Bruffin, got to make it up with Bruffin." Max woke mouthing the words not kindly but with immense cunning. One more move like that and the game was his. Of course, they made no more sense than most dream thoughts. "You can't be reborn without making it up with Bruffin." His receding astral self sniggered and disappeared.

After breakfast, he started another column. And he felt more than before a cringing urge to ingratiate. *Marbles* is not such a bad play, really; actually, it is contemptible, but why say so? Probably produced by a group of lonely people, out scouring the countryside for their lost children. A bad review in *Now* would be the last straw.

"*Marbles* has at least good intentions." Yes, the intentions of clearing expenses, conning the public, and soothing the backers. Still, fat little men with cigars have to live, too. They have children to look for. He unrolled the paper and started again. "*Marbles* is a load of vicious crap. The people who made it have boils in their armpits"—no, that's me. Max is getting bored now. If you don't watch out, he is going to die of boredom.

He typed, Chinese style, chop-chop with two fingers, a thoroughly insipid review. He wheeled it over to *Now* and dumped it. Maybe his mail contained some invitations to parties. A reception for Polish filmmakers would be just perfect. Foreign accents kept your mind occupied. Trying to speak French to a bunch of Poles or Lithuanians. What a mind-blower that would be.

As he sat at his desk, running his forefinger through the envelopes and throwing away the contents, he began to feel guilty about his column. You'll get fired for this one for sure. He had written it with splendid lassitude; but now that he was in the plant, he found himself accepting the importance of *Now*. He thought of trying to rewrite it, with biting jokes and whatnot. But then thought, You're a grown-up now, Jamison. Biting jokes are high school. Criticism is high school.

He craved company, any company. So he went out in the hallway and skimmed the neighboring cubicles. Everybody was serenely occupied. Inwardly, they pulsated with grief, he could tell. At night, they cried themselves to sleep. Huge, flailing editors, moaning like babies, their thumbs in their mouths. Talented researchers, spraddled in corners, empty gin bottles dripping down their laps. But here they were all very neat in their white shirts and their quiet, medium-length dresses.

Don Ferris in books might be a bet. His reading must keep him in some touch with chaos. Max sauntered in. He was not usually clubbable, so a visit from him would be a surprise to anyone.

"Hi, Max. You want to do a book?" Ferris looked as if he'd never heard of chaos.

"Not specially. You got anything good?"

"Oh Christ." Ferris waved at his assembly line. "Who knows?" He rolled his chair toward them, like a wheelchair, and began thumbing. *50 Years in the Theater* by Eli Griswold. How does that grab you?"

Max shook his head. He thought of four or five jokes about Griswold, but was too tired to make any of them. The whole joke culture was a screaming bore anyway. Why didn't people in New York just admit they hated each other and snarl and tear at each other's eyes? Instead of making jokes that nobody wanted to hear? "Griswold's a nice old man," he found himself saying incredibly. "I wouldn't want to hurt his feelings."

"Well, then. There's *Theatre Dynamics* by Heinrich Fuller."

Six more jokes were rejected out of hand. Fuller was one of the new strippers: a fat little man who took off his clothes and rolled around the stage, jeering at the audience. "Your bodies are dead," Fuller would scream, his little penis flapping. "Your souls are dead men's shit." Very funny fellow. Max just shook his head.

"What about some allied field? We've got some stuff on the New Film, the meaning of silence in Jerry Lewis, Godard's use of the tit . . ."

Please don't be so lively. I'm an old man, a very old man. You don't have to make jokes if you don't want to. Ferris was not one of your natural funsters, but a solemn young fellow from Antioch; but he twittered along anyway, in the compulsory joke language.

Look, Don. Just tell me how I'm doing. Is the work all right? Oh yes, Max, the work is fine. Haven't you noticed it falling off lately? No, Max, I haven't noticed the work falling off . . . Then, a minute later, Don would send a call through to the board room. "Max was in here just now. I think he's slipping, as you requested. He asked me how he was doing." Heads nodding. A trip to Japan by slumber jet for Max.

You couldn't confide in anyone here. Don Ferris seemed friendly enough, but whose side was he really on? A young egghead working for *Now* must be pretty depraved. *Now* might be all right for old men with families to support, all right for King Lear or Jamison, but not you, you little ass-licker, shitface—Max stood up and said, "Not today, Don, thanks all the same."

He went back for one more tilt with *Marbles*. He tried to set his mind, as one sets a typewriter. Why are *you* doing this, King Jamison? To make money, to support my ungrateful family. The old king slips it under the portcullis: greedy hands at the other side, pouncing on it like ferrets. Old King Jamison wanders off through the snow, hitching at his gown.

The hell with *Marbles*. And yet he didn't want to lose his damn job. The less the work meant, the more important it seemed to hang on to it. To be fired now, from this worthless task—why, they'll have to cut the uniform off me, sir.

He had to see Harvey Salter to find out if the column was O.K. With a muffled groan, he got up from his desk. The spiritual life had left him scuffling over the daily bread quite hilariously. No wonder the church was so corrupt. "How'm I doing, column O.K.?" He mouthed the words casually, not believing for a moment that this was Max Jamison.

When he got out in the hall, his pride rushed back to his head. A physical matter, some slight stirring in the ego glands, caused by standing up quickly. A couple of secretaries went giggling past. Grab one quickly and force-feed your confidence with that, my boy. Critics should be fed young girls from time to time; virgins should be flung into their cages. Otherwise, they became wall-eyed spinsters. Petulant, fearful. They should also wrestle in mud and swat each other with bags of shit, for manliness. Then go off somewhere and pray.

"How's it going, Max?" Bathe in asses' milk, don lily-white robes . . .

"O.K." Who was that? Never mind. They're all alike.

He went back to his desk more cheerfully. If he looked at the mirror, he would see that the top of his head was missing, and that green fur had sprouted in the ruins. But he wasn't going to look. What he was going to do was go to a party, any party, and get smashed and find some mind-obliterating woman and lose himself the old way. Opening his mind, free-associating, had simply released this thin trickle of pus.

There was nothing else there, honestly. No sun and moon. Just a few obscenities, a little can of hatred, rotting stumps, like bad teeth, of fantasy. And even that was a fake. Not the free flow of a psychotic, but energetic invention. The priesthood indeed! Who had put that idea there? Why, Max Jamison himself. He used to compare criticism with the priesthood. One of his best gags. Subconscious? In a pig's eye. He had laid waste to that years ago, used what he could and boarded up the rest. You may think Max is pouring out his soul, but do not be deceived. He is pouring out memory, second-rate fiction, bad poetry.

In this really happy mood, Max did go to a party, completely his old self, socked the host, almost breaking his jaw, tried to lug one of the female guests into the bathroom, and passed out with his head in the toilet, his hair dangling like seaweed.

part four

21

Helen felt as if she was recuperating from a disease, or an exorcism. You did not remove someone like Max with simple surgery. Once the body was out, you scoured the remains with candles, burning away live tissue. Anything he had touched, bits of heart, scraps of nerve must go. Months had gone by since he left and she felt that the evil spirit was lifting at last. But you couldn't be too careful.

Gene Mungo was vastly tolerant. He saw nothing intrinsically wrong with the idea of Max Jamison—Max was entitled to his thing as much as anyone else. If his thing included rage at Gene Mungo, O.K., man. Hope it helps. His own thing was *not* to have standards. Helen was relaxing and growing under his care. Nothing ever grew under Max. Your mind didn't grow while you were watching your grammar. Your mind didn't grow if you weren't allowed to use words like "grow." (Tacky abstractions, Max called them.)

Her days were dreamy. Gene would mooch about the kitchen covered in paint, chewing things, or stand in the garden waiting for his pot to grow, not straining himself. She could run a slatternly house for him, leaving dishes in the sink for three days and beds unmade. He didn't drink and was slapdash about his eating: none of Max's punctilio. If supper wasn't there by ten o'clock, he opened a can of peaches.

"I needed this," she said, rooting a hand under his shirt. "I'd forgotten that freedom existed. My husband was like a courtroom that was always in session."

"He's happy," said Gene, sprawled in his basic position, satirically supine, on the double bed. "You won't get that freedom you want if you keep on thinking about him."

"Should I tell him to stop sending his checks?" she asked solemnly.

"Shit, I didn't say you had to go to extremes."

"Take sex," she said.

"Yeah." He stretched his legs.

"Even there, he had standards. He didn't mention them but they were there, all right. You felt he was going to write a review about it. 'A thoroughly disappointing intercourse. Helen Jamison performed like a rank amateur. The climax was a bomb.'"

"You're crazy. He didn't think that stuff. *You* did."

"Maybe. And I'll tell you something else I thought. I thought deep down he was a sadist. He wanted to hurt me. God, the bruises on my arms and legs. I looked like a football player."

"Let me see." He pretended to examine, got absorbed. But she kept talking. "I'm convinced what he really wanted to do was beat me. Beat me senseless. But his moral code wouldn't allow it. That's why he was never satisfied, that's why he kept looking for new women."

"Very ingenious." Gene's voice was muffled. "Them he beat?"

"I don't suppose so. That's nice, Gene. No, I don't think he did."

"One way and another, I'm getting pretty tired of him. O.K. if we change the subject?"

"O.K."

But not for long. She had to scrape Max from her system. "You liked him once"—yes, that was true. Liked him, used him, learned from him. Then one night she looked at his face and couldn't stand it any longer. A post-lecture night. He was breathing over her, his big features pulsing with rage which he mistook for desire, his fingers digging at her shoulder blades like a cop making an arrest. You have exceeded the speed limit, you have gone through a red light. Pull over and lie down. Even in this paroxysm, he was judging her.

Max, get off a minute and let's talk. I know you don't think I'm very bright, whatever you say, but I think I'm on to something. Max would accept a good idea from the grocer. He ravened for intelligence. If she saw something wrong with him he would want to know about it. He had a big thing on honesty.

Honesty! He sat up flustered, pajama tops gaping. She had overestimated his pride ridiculously. He had practically none at all. Fancy thinking he could take criticism. Instead he lashed back like a wounded play and whipped her to ribbons with his wit.

He sat beside her on the bed, twisting a button until it came off in his fingers, and she thought of a dying bull, hurt, baffled, but lunging at the pain with his horns; in his case, with phrases, brilliant formulas. He didn't believe in himself, but, my God, he could make a case for himself.

Everything she said after that made it harder to say the next thing. Until she too was hitting blindly, attacking the good things about him as well as the others, making his work seem like a monstrosity and, in the heat of war, believing it, as one believes the silliest propaganda in wartime.

Now, slowly, Gene was cooling her, bringing her to a rational acceptance of Max. He was still the father of her children, Gene pointed out, and she could not be completely rid of him. Perhaps in a few more weeks she should write him a friendly note, inviting him up.

Justin did seem to miss his father, if listlessness was anything to go by (or was listlessness correct at his age?). He did not care for Gene at all, and managed to avoid him even in a small house. It was all the same to Charlie, one big hairy presence was like another, but Justin had somehow turned against both men, and showed it by becoming fat and slovenly. With his mother, he had adopted a rather artificial charm and animation. When she tried to probe his feelings, he changed the subject to food. Or just stood opening and shutting the icebox door. So perhaps she should try to bring him back together with Max, when she could face it herself.

This was her mood when the first letter arrived from Max, accusing her of destroying him, sprinkling her with obscenities, and demanding custody of the children immediately.

The first effect of this was a deeper dreaminess. She assembled her scenes for the lawyer. Wondered if Max remembered the same things. For instance, her days teaching at the Gotham School of Social Research, helping to support them both. Max's job at *Rearview* paid practically nothing, and the checks from his father were small and embarrassing. There was a myth that Max was self-sufficient and that her job was an amusing do-good trifle. He poked mild fun at her social conscience. They lived a huge big lie about money, and the lie had this anti-feminist sub-clause. Anything he did was important, anything she did was a hobby.

Of course, you couldn't work long at the Gotham School without developing a social conscience. But she couldn't seem to convince Max that this was a real thing, based on real children, and not some form of hot flashes. His faint smile as she talked to guests about it, his "What did you do at school today, dear" tone, made clear who handled the real work around here.

Guests, yes. Let's take a look at Max the host. The Smithers are coming to dinner tonight. Hurry back from school and be hostess. Vivian Smithers is a great admirer of Max's. Bob Smithers is very quiet but almost certainly admires him too. Max will, does, enter the living room talking. Vivian Smithers loves his latest thing. Bob hasn't read it yet. ("Bob hasn't read anything yet," Max will say later.)

Max accepts the compliment, confesses he rather liked the piece himself. Bob is dying to read it. Helen is in and out of the kitchen, trying to keep up with the conversation. Bob is getting so little of it, having read nothing and seen nothing, that she is embarrassed for him and tries to work him in. But Bob is an intellectual eunuch, with little fat hips on his soul. Sorry, but that's the way she sees him. A ghastly couple, when you stop to think of it.

"Excuse me for interrupting, but dinner's ready."

Max looks up, irritated, and glares at her briefly as if she were a pushy waitress. But he gets up swiftly and finishes his joke. Enters the next room laughing.

The dinner is a Max performance. You can't precisely say that he's showing off, because if he didn't talk tonight, nobody would. She is tired and flustered from cooking and having taken the subway from school and having shopped on the way home, and would like somebody to say something about that. Max prides himself on being a gourmet, but often fails to mention the food. Maybe that means he doesn't like it.

"I'm afraid the beans are overcooked," Helen says desperately, introducing the subject by main force.

Max smiles. "They're not and you know it. And it's a great meal." Murmurs of "Excellent" from the Smithers, and Vivian asks wanly about the recipe. Max does not act bored, but she feels that she must get the kitchen talk over with as quickly as possible and get back to him. They have only been married two years at this

208

point, and she respects his priorities. She stumbles over her words, and leaves out the lemon, and Vivian, without writing anything down, says, "I've got to try it." And then Max comes barreling in with his latest theatrical adventure and that's the end of that.

Why does he have such unintelligent friends? No, they're not unintelligent. They are quick, responsive— Max demands intelligence. But then he won't let them use it. He sits on their tiny heads and won't let them breathe. She is awfully tired of theater talk and would like to bring up a boy called Manny Rodriguez who has written a surprisingly good poem about Mars. But she pictures Max smiling and waiting for her to get through, and she doesn't tell it. Her work is precious to her; and Manny's poem should not be subjected to super-critic.

Max has dealt the cards and named the game. It is called "Criticism."

"I disagreed with Max about *Last Thursday*," she says at last. "I thought he was a bit unkind to it."

"Kindness is wasted on plays. Unless you include mercy killing."

Oh, don't be such a smarty-pants. Dear. "The people in the play are the kind of Americans I grew up with in Indiana. Perhaps . . ."

"Well, I see you left Indiana," he interrupts. "I don't know why you want it following you here."

"I must say, it sounds kind of dreary," says Vivian Smithers.

Helen suddenly feels like screaming. Who are you to sneer at Indiana? Do you think you are so wonderfully interesting? Do you think your own lives are such mar-

vels of subtlety and grace? We'll except Max for now—
he is sneering from strength. She admires Max. But the
Smithers are average, timid, unoriginal New Yorkers,
miming their superiors, lacking in moral courage, imagination and I don't know, everything.

Max can usually read her more violent thoughts.
"They're probably good people, dear, but you know you
were bored by them yourself. Is it really fair to inflict
them on us?"

"I guess not." Boss. Repeat. They have been married
two years. Later on she would tackle him in an open
field. She wouldn't care how smart he was. Reckless,
suicidal, she would fling herself on him. But in those
early days she is still afraid to take him on, especially in
front of other people. He has no compunction about hu-
miliating her, or anyone. "Ideas have rights," he says.

She serves a mousse that hasn't worked out too well,
although Bob Smithers raves about it now that he is
started. Max has told her not to apologize for things, it
only makes them worse, so she says no more and simply
waits for everyone to leave.

So that is the first thing she thought about when she
got the letter. "I hate to say it, but wasn't the sauce too
thin?" Was she destroying him that night, or later?

Some years after that, Max the guest. Everything
more so than it used to be, the vanity more ruthless, the
desire for love more unscrupulous. Or is it only that she
sees more? Will these scenes stand up in a court of law?

The Weinbergs are more advanced than the Smithers. They put on a show of resistance, throw out an oc-

casional glove. Excellent. Max prances gorgeously. Mr. Weinberg says, "I've only seen two Albee plays . . ."

"I didn't know there *were* two," says Max. Laughter. "Barely one act." Hy Weinberg is an excellent ball boy, a psychiatrist with an interest in the arts. The kind of person they seem to see a lot of now.

"The characters in Albee are really all men, aren't they?" asks Mabel Weinberg.

"I wouldn't say *that* exactly," says Max. Pauses. Laughter. "No, not exactly that." Hy scoops up the glasses. They have reached the stage in life where you don't have to peep at the host's bottles before you order your drink. You know he has everything. Nor will you have to gag down bad California wine. You still do when you dine with the Jamisons, but not when the Jamisons dine with you. That's integrity for you.

"How many plays has Tennessee Williams written?"

"Ah, these Southern belles. Let me see now. One, one and a half, one and three quarters—I would say about two and a third altogether. *Menagerie on a Hot Tin Streetcar.*"

Have I started to destroy you yet? Helen is bored, of course. Husband's jokes are for export only, after the first year or so. But it is worse than that. She is now judging Max by his own standards. And by those standards, he is mediocre. His jokes smell of the carpentry shop. You can see the joins, the place where A is inserted into B. And Max delivers them like someone who's hung around too many theaters, sort of a road-company Oscar Wilde. Fair comment, right, Max?

Max does not flirt with Mabel. God forbid. Mabel

looks as if she could use a meal. And she has a Bronx accent. But there is a girl along, there is always a girl along. One of those vague, pretty girls who land on New York like moths and flutter off again after a year or two, leaving a few small holes in various lives. Assistant editor at *Clothes Horse* or *Women Arise* or somewhere. Would like Max to do a piece on our changing theater. They will talk about this later. Perhaps over lunch. Perhaps over breakfast.

Max plays to her, dedicates the applause and heartaches. Helen is so tired of the standard New York dinner, the bring your drinks to the table, the stay and finish your wine, the would you like brandy or B & B. As rigid as the standard New York restaurant, with the bar and the red banquettes. Funeral parlors for funeral ceremonies. Max sneered at Helen's "love of life"—but look at the alternative.

Max shows off like a dynamo now, a machine for showing off, right through dinner and drinks. There is no point in her listening, but he wants her to listen. She is his trainer, his lucky hunchback. Afterwards, he will sniff around for her approval. Was he funny tonight, has he still got it? She must signal assent with an extra kick of the legs, a low moan of homage. Landing the assistant editor of *Clothes Horse* some time hence will be all right in its way, but no substitute for approval from the coach.

You see I was in a pretty bad way, she said to herself. I had to leave. *Destroy* such a man? You have to be joking.

Max had continued their sex life long after it ceased

having erotic content, simply to give *her* a chance to applaud him. The faceless pretties that he bucked and hammered against were the new generation and had to be impressed too; but she was his beginnings, she was the red schoolhouse where they kept the standards. Sex was just a metaphor for how'm I doing?

—"Don't you see, Gene—it doesn't matter whether he was like that or not. So long as I thought he was, I couldn't live with him."

"He says in the letter, no more money?"

"That's right." She looked at Gene questioningly. He never pretended to be anything but a rogue and an opportunist. On the other hand, his actual living expenses came to about $300 a year, so he didn't do it for money. He grinned. "Old Max can't get away with that." Gene rolled over and his lids shut like a doll's.

How'm I doing and take that, you bitch, and rotten performance, my pet. Max couldn't be saying all that every time he made love. Perhaps she had been getting hysterical. Even the God of Calvin never judged anyone as harshly as married couples judged each other.

Yet here was his letter, foaming, whining, drenched in some foul liquid. It made her tremble just to hold it. Had he gone crazy or what? It was like something out of hell. She felt she ought to burn it by moonlight. But Gene just thought it was funny. "It's good for him," he said. "Get all that stuff out of his system. He'll never feel better till he gets rid of that stuff."

"You think so, O sage?"

"Sure. It's like a fever. You can't have a conversion without falling off your horse. You can't get well without first a sickness. Otherwise, you wouldn't recognize health when you saw it. Hey—he writes well, doesn't he?"

Gene was a great comfort. But she didn't quite believe him. To her, Max was coming into his own now; the letters were what he had really meant to say all along. She could just hear him adding, "Mungo's formulas are as symmetrical and well-rounded as his head. Up down, sick well, ah so." A perverse thought: She suddenly wished Max approved of Gene. You could trust him to be fair about a thing like that. And it would certainly help her life with Gene. Max was, for what it was worth, one of the best critics in America.

22

Justin's point of view was that he was just in it for the food. He did not concern himself about domestic arrangements, except as they affected the food supply: supper was likely to be later these days, and the icebox was less predictable. On the other hand, he was allowed to use it more than ever. In the dimly remembered old days the clunk of the door often aroused his father from the next room, and a shout of "Justin? What the hell are you doing in there?" would smash it shut.

Dim, unreliable memories. Daddy was the man who kept you from getting to the food. Then later, in an unaccountable reverse, Daddy became the soft touch, the gateway to hotdogs and chocolate milk shakes, Mr. Peanut, the gingerbread man. Justin never trusted the change. At some minute, while his cheeks were full, the old man would sneak up and start beating him with the stick which Justin imagined was concealed at all times in his father's trouser leg. It was a test of courage asking for food, a means of telling if one's magic held.

Max had not actually beaten his children with anything. Better he had. They would have discovered the limit to his strength. As it was, Justin imagined lightning darting from that stick, thorns that gouged like nails, and a roaring sound that kept growing to infinity. Max had a big personality for a father and with the best will in the world couldn't help frightening his kids.

Justin, that is; not Charlie. Charlie's manifest courage had already begun to bug Justin. Nobody else knew it, but Justin had tried to frighten his brother a few times, to establish a hierarchy of fear in the family. He had threatened various succulent tortures that Charlie probably hadn't the imagination to picture yet, had teased him in ways that he, Justin, wouldn't admit to anybody and had wound up locking him in the broom closet. The best he could get was something that could only be called "brave tears." After which, he was afraid of Charlie, too.

So things were pretty fat and glum right now. He feared his father's return more than anything, feared the big voice and the magic rod. Justin was King of the Kitchen at least, but his father might dispute even that and drive him from his lands. The new guy was pretty much of a jerk, though he might turn on you, too. The thing could probably be managed, if he kept in good with his mother.

An even dimmer memory was that he loved his father, and would die to please him. Those were the tears marked meaningless. Whatever exchange they were based on—squinting at Max from the crib and seeing him upside down, learning to walk with his hands safely in his father's, feeling the house was all right for the night when he heard Max's voice next door—was long since gone. The couple of times he cried at night were honestly over nothing.

It wasn't just food of course; Justin just thought it was. Helen knew better. What it was was that Max had turned his love, which meant his full attention, on the boy and crushed him.

"You're nuts," said Gene.

"No, that's exactly what happened. Max's love contained so much hostility . . ."

"Did you talk to *him* like this?"

"Yes, I guess so."

"No wonder he's gone crazy."

Helen felt blinded. Then she said, "*He* taught me to see things like that. He taught me how to criticize. I never used to before . . ."

"Look," said Gene. "You want to talk about Max, you'd better live with Max. He probably enjoys it more than I do."

"I'm sorry."

Gene rolled over on his stomach. She wondered whether years from now she would even be able to remember what he looked like upright. "You understand, *I* can't help him," he said. "It's also my personal opinion that *you* can't help him."

217

"True."

"I'll tell you what you do, then. First you shut up. O.K.? Then you decide what's best for the kid, and just do it. Keeping your mouth firmly shut at all times."

"But that's what I can't decide, you see. Justin may need a father, but he hated seeing Max. He used to say, 'I won't see him, I'm going to a friend's.' He couldn't stand Max after Max left us."

"I swore I wouldn't get into this. But how about *before* Max left us?"

"That was a little better. Seeing Max all the time, he was a little less alarming for the children. It's these sudden doses that are hard to take."

"Boy, you have made some kind of monster out of Max, and probably passed him on to the kids in that form, too. He is, folks, in real life a normal sort of guy, clean, well-spoken, snappy dresser. Tries to make jokes, some good, some so-so. Doesn't get too sore if they don't work."

"You could drive people crazy with just those qualities."

"I like Max. He's honest. He calls me a racketeer to my face. You don't have to worry about what he says behind your back, because there's nothing left to say."

"You have just described a prize boor."

"No, I know it's his job, being rude. Of course, he doesn't know shit about art. His soul is a genuine antique. Christ, I can't even talk to the guy about that. I mean, the words are O.K., but the thoughts are granny's specials. Once more, now, Christ and Amen. I now declare this subject closed forever."

"Don't you ever get tired of doing this?"

"What?"

"This."

"Christ, I hope not."

"Quit following me," said Justin. Charlie grinned, and when Justin moved, he moved too. "Look, I said quit following me." Charlie grinned some more. He could follow you for three days in the desert, if he put his mind to it. Justin gave him a push. Charlie fell back a step and waited.

"What do you want?" Charlie knew how to speak, but seldom used the privilege. He stood welded to a stubborn patch of snow, definitely the last for this winter, grinning like a maniac. Knocking him into the snow seemed like a good idea, so Justin rushed him again. But Charlie had a crazy center of gravity: standing and sitting were virtually the same thing to him. He did not exactly go down.

Justin considered really belting him, but saw that it would do no good. Charlie was crazy and you couldn't hurt him. Next Justin thought of bribery. Straight cash? Charlie was a cheap pay-off, because he didn't know a dime from a penny. But this time he shook his head. Toys? Justin had already handed over most of these. Creative playthings lay piled like bomb damage in the cellar. "You want my football? I hate it." Charlie shook his head again.

Finally, Justin just turned and ran. When he peeped back over his shoulder, he saw that his younger brother was jogging along in grave pursuit. There was no escaping him. Justin wasn't bored, he was terrified. A silver-bullet wouldn't do a thing for Charlie except possibly encourage him. Justin lost him in the lane in back of the house, but he would be waiting.

The next letter from Max threatened to come and rip up the place, smash the chairs and pull her hair out by the roots. Gene roared over it. "I can't help liking that man," he said. Helen was more alarmed than ever. Max was a man of stern self-control. If he took his hand away, his stomach would fall out—that kind of control.

"He has to be kidding this time," said Gene. "You can hear him cackle between the lines."

She read it again, and she could indeed hear the cackle, and the sound of bat wings in the chimney too, but couldn't see how this helped. If Max had decided to unrein his vast hatred on the world, this would not preclude humor. Max's humor was a collection of switchblades, blackjacks, and homemade bombs.

"You think he's serious?"

"Oh yes. If Max says he's going to do something, he'll do it."

"You mean, we should put up barricades, start drilling in the basement?"

"I don't know, I don't know." She gave an isolated sob. "Max could beat you to death for a gag. That I'm sure of."

"It's all in your head, possum. Just because he frightened you intellectually, you've turned him into a Gila monster. American women just can't take it."

"Can't take what?"

"The full force of the male mind. It makes them hallucinate."

Well, that was true. She dreamed that night of a

bloated, hairy Max raging around New York, chewing furniture, yanking out fixtures, working his way slowly North—finally looming over the house like King Kong; carrying her off to some seminar; and raping her senseless while he explained the decline of the drama. She woke up with fists beating the sheet. I've got to stop him sending those letters. Her system would never expel him if he was allowed to make these outrageous intrusions.

But another one came, threatening her with a savage beating, and another after that with actual death. She didn't like to call the police, not on the boys' father, and she didn't want to throw the letters away unopened. Occasionally they contained checks, which she unfortunately needed—made out neatly for generous amounts —and once she had got that far, she could hardly keep from reading the accompanying text. Sometimes Gene beat her to it, grabbing the letter and howling with glee. "Your husband is really some fantastic writer," he said. "Do you know what the bugger has in mind for you today? You won't believe it. What imagination, what style. Boy, I dig this man all the way."

Although indications were that Max was not planning a real visit, she still felt physically threatened by the letters: somehow as if he had actually done these things to her, all the times he had looked as if he meant to. This of course made no sense to Gene, who continued to whoop simple-heartedly over the letters and was, truth to tell, beginning to annoy her in that respect.

23

It was intolerably sentimental to see any hope at all in his particular life. The rage Max spent every night in these senseless letters to women was just enough to keep him sane, but that was all. Hobbling down to the mailbox like a cripple (that's how he saw himself), limping and listing on no fixed principle, jamming the letters into the flapping mailbox mouth, as though to break teeth, and hobbling up again to his apartment to sleep.

It was a funny set of spiritual exercises, not one recommended by the great masters, but it worked. It got him to the office in the mornings, kept him writing his meaningless pieces, kept him out of ugly scenes with doormen. Oh yes, it worked—but there was no *hope* in it. No more for him than for the old man crouched in the john writing hopeless messages to the world about the size of his prick, or the dwarf foaming and dripping into some poor girl's telephone, or any of his blood brothers, his gibbering, club-footed co-religionists.

He had pried his spirit open, after all, breaking twelve locks and a crowbar, and this is what he had found there. Yes, I just stumbled upon this little religion by chance. I was writing a simple note to the wife when it just came to me. Why not put a little sulphur in your life? It didn't seem like my kind of thing at first, I mean, it's kind of undignified, isn't it, a bit on the primitive side. But brothers and sisters, it works. It *works*. It brings peace to your empty heart, smooths the wrinkles in your scrotum, gets a body out of himself.

He could think like that as he wrote—his letters to Eve were particularly zesty. But afterwards he was shrunken and paralytic. Not guilty, not right then, but very tired and ready for sleep. The next day, he would go to screenings or his office at *Now,* and work with spiritless craft. He had accumulated enough technique over the years to conceal the state of his soul from the sharpest reader. And God knows, the competition in his field was weak enough. He could write at half strength and still be better than most of them. So long as he could just work on his letters at night, he didn't worry much about his days. His paranoia about *Now* cleared up like a minor infection: they were soft, affable people who wouldn't hurt you because they couldn't bear to be hurt themselves. Paternal organizations were built on great piles of spiritual blubber.

He didn't, during these lucid indifferent hours, think

coherently about the night. This new vice was so out-landish that there wasn't much to think about anyway; he just went home blindly and did it. Consequences. There would be none. Women liked to be frightened. They would read the letters as crazy declarations of love. Women could plow anything into love, bless them.

Good, fine girls, his ex-students. Always happy to hear from the old prof, to be sure. Then for a few min-utes just before waking, he would hear from the other side. His dreams would roll into a fist and pound him. He used to be a big man in his own dreams, a god; he had always routed his pursuers and forced the ecto-plasm into worshipful shapes. But those days were gone. He now appeared in various cruddy guises: an old man creeping alongside a fence urinating into his hat; an old actor with a skin disease, whose pants kept fall-ing down; a dead man being rowed out to sea and dumped, in a bag marked *New York A.C.* All clearly understood to be Max Jamison. So he had his *modus vivendi*, but absolutely no hope.

The worst and commonest dream had the police breaking in the door to find him asprawl among his foul-smelling chemicals. "Kiss me, sergeant," he would say to complete his degradation. Or other times he would get all the way to magistrates court and receive a lecture vaguely as follows. "Of all the vile, unspeakable prac-tices that this bench has ever encountered . . ." Max leans forward as his honor gropes in his pants like a bur-lesque clown. ". . . Of all the rotten festering occupa-tions . . ." The guardian of the law has almost pulled himself onto the floor by now; but in the nick of time, whips out, triumphantly—a Max Jamison review.

Pandemonium. Women throw up. The windows are lined like the deck of a channel steamer with retching, shuddering backs. Jamison goes on his way.

The question of whether to use the letters for instruction was a knotty one. These girls still had a lot to learn. But he wondered if teaching wasn't bad for *him*. It was known to be a perverse activity. *Teaching as perversion* would be a good title for his autobiography. Corrupting the youth. Come here, my dear, and let me show you something. Knowledge, yum-yum. A lifetime of that would make anyone sick. Pre-frontal gonorrhea from intercourse with too many young minds. That lump on the end of my nose that I can't see past—ah-hah. Cranial clap. I've been sticking it into those young minds again. He signed the letter, then with his arm still full of jism decided to add a postscript.

Lash them instead, my dear, tell them nothing. No one ever got a disease from using a whip. "Eve, you sweet little cunt, humping your way through New York arts and letters, filled to the brim with the juice of your betters: juice that you are too stingy and stupid to use." Notice how instruction creeps in? He was aiming in his new art for the perfectly neutral insult, the kind that implied no course of improvement. But there was always this element of "why don't you just . . ." It was something to work on, in the foul late hours.

Eve cried over the letters, simply and long, and felt angry at life for doing these things to people. She had only been in love twice in her life, and each time the man had cracked up, for all her careful handling. Her husband had turned homosexual after a long course in booze—something she hadn't told Max about, out of embarrassment. She had tried being soft with Harold, tried being hard; passive, aggressive, girlish, boyish, anything he wanted. And he had turned down the full range of feminine wares and had chosen instead a red-headed half-wit from somebody's shipping department.

Shattering. By the time she got to Max, she didn't know quite what to do with a man. This big love-starved peacock couldn't be *that* hard to please—but she had no confidence in her methods. She smiled too slowly (was that what he wanted?), gave the wrong answers, worried about bed. All the things he didn't need as he rumbled toward his crack-up. And why had she said that about his children? Only because she was scared of them. It was nerve-racking enough being right for Max. But when he began to notice that she read aloud to his kids in a silly voice and made inferior brownies, it would just be too much.

So she went through the letters carefully. Max's fantasies about her empty heart—oh God, empty!—and her overflowing bed. She might have hoped for better judgment from a critic, even a crazy one. She had slept with nobody since he left, and was only hoping to pull herself together someday soon. Naturally, she blamed herself for Max's state. It would have been a pleasure to help him. A good man, by her standards, fair and honest. There was no jealousy or smallness about him. He even praised his enemies when they called for it, without spite or calculation: which made him almost unique in New York circles, where praise was part of your climbing equipment. She didn't mind his arrogance a bit. By some accident of upbringing, he thought it was all right to say what was on his mind. In a town teeming with ego, Max could almost classify as humble. Of all the people she knew here, Max was also the only one who seemed physically incapable of lying.

It added up to an obliterating sense of loss. Max with his Roman virtues was just what she needed in this tinny town. Who would suppose he would care so much about his children? Or was that just more Roman virtue? It didn't matter. Honor was a kind of passion. Integrity was a passion. Let no one say that a man like that had no feelings.

Well—all gone now. She had hoped until the letters that he would call again and she would act with a little more firmness and clarity next time. But there was no returning to a man who had said those things to you. Even if you didn't mind the things in themselves, as she in truth didn't, Max himself would be huge with shame when he returned to his senses.

Poor old Max. She would keep in touch through his writing. It seemed to her a small miracle that he kept that up as well as he did. But it seemed softer and kinder than it used to. More descriptive, and less eager to criticize. Alas, not as good. More ingratiating: almost in some ways to be asking forgiveness. She hoped it was helping him. This was no world for New England Calvinists.

The only one who seriously thought of calling the police was Max's first wife, Georgette. She had scores to settle with Max, skin burns and lacerations that had never healed. His scorn for her conversational powers had left Georgette with something between a straight stammer and a kind of stumbling rush that got her syllables in the wrong order. She made a joke of it, the old "clever woman being silly" joke, but black sweat poured out of her brain. And now he was back, pulling her nerves out and tying granny knots in them.

She put it to her husband, Terence, as a matter of civic duty. But Terence put it back to her as a matter of scandal. He assumed that anything reported to the police would turn up on the front pages of the nation immediately, that five-part series about it would begin to sprout in all the magazines, and that Otto Preminger would start work on the movie version shortly. If you married a man as different as possible from your previous husband, you had to take the consequences and Terence was the consequences. Besides, there was some question about what the police in Palo Alto, California, could do about letters datemarked New York City anyway.

So Max was spared the midnight visitation of the fuzz. And as his letters received no response at all, they drifted closer toward a diary. He began to discuss in them *why* he was writing them in the first place, a complicated artistic form which required a different and saner brand of energy. Thus criticism crept back into his work.

Private criticism. Of his public criticism, suffice it to say that he got a letter from Reginald Leroy, the most vivacious producer on Broadway, to say how much he had enjoyed Max's recent work with its accent on the positive; Leroy's people had actually been able to use some quotes from *Now* lately, "and believe me, Max, this is good for the theater and good for all of us."

Yes, Max knew what this meant, just as he knew what the fat-faced grins meant on opening night, the arm on the shoulder and the fatherly pinch on the elbow: an elbow they wouldn't have touched once upon a time. It was a sweet weak feeling like recovering from pneumonia. The technical name for this feeling was "power." Max had become a force on Broadway. Warren Beckley, the fag director, told him so over lunch. In his weakened condition, Max found this rather amusing.

24

Helen said, "It's not that funny." Gene's thigh slapping seemed contrived today. He looked at the letter again and said, "You're right." Max's latest was pretty boring. All about the place of scatology in Western culture, the need to express the Dionysian, etc. It was like an archaeology professor discovering jazz. "He'll never get it, will he?" Gene hit his guitar, which he used mainly for punctuational effects. "I liked him the way he was before. You don't meet that many good grandfather clocks these days."

"Look, would you mind either learning that instrument or giving it to the Salvation Army? And also, how about standing up so I can make the bed?"

"Pleasure."

The joys of living with a slob were less keen on some days than on others. Maybe, somewhere, a thoughtful slob was waiting: a man who lived simply but cleaned up after himself. She didn't think it was of major importance, but the reek of Mungo's arm and leg pits was pretty damn dizzying today. As soon as she had flattened the sheets and blankets, he was back on them.

"Do you do this to make a point?"

"What's that, honey?"

"All this lying about."

"Point? Me?"

"Yes. Make. Point. You."

"Huh. I guess I should have told you sooner—I don't dig gentle criticism, that 'you can pull out my toenail if I can pull out yours' crap. Didn't your marriage teach you where that stuff leads?"

He shut his eyes, then reached blindly for his cigarette. This love of life seemed to require a lot of rest. As he lay there, puffy, stinking, smug, she couldn't help seeing him through Max's eyes for a second. One of the new fakers, living off the fat of the public's head. He had done two paintings since they got up here, which had taken about two hours apiece. Otherwise, he lay around like a greedy child, reaching for her as if she was candy.

She kissed him gently and smiled. Max's poor crazy eyes were not much to look through nowadays. His long earnest letter, defending the need for obscenity "in a healthy mind," and almost forgetting to swear himself, was drained of terror for her. The thing is, Max, I was right, wasn't I? I said you couldn't go on the way you were going. No one can be that stiff and holy. I'm not saying I told you so—but I had to get away from that, didn't I?

All right, just say that Gene is built for the 1970's and leave it at that. If this was 1890, it might be altogether different. You would be just the thing, Max.

To which the old Max, dead now except in memory, said, "Balls. He fits the 1970's the way a whore fits the soldiers." You know, if Max stops being himself, I will be the only person left who can still think like Max? I'll be an author's widow, and literary executor, for the whole last part of his life.

While she was thinking like this, or some other way— for hours passed in this house now, unaccounted for— she heard a hideous crash and a wail. She snapped awake and followed the noise. Down in the kitchen, her sons were confronting each other. Charles was bleary-eyed, like a silent comedian who has walked into a glass door. Justin had a baseball bat in his hand.

"What happened? I told you not to bring that in here," she screamed.

There was an enormous purple bruise on Charlie's shin, but he wasn't the one who was crying. He was the stoical side of Max, the one that no letter, no threat, could touch. Justin, the critic, dropped his bat and flung himself at her legs, howling.

Late May and the last round-up of the campus dollar. Max had been accepting lecture engagements raven-ously. He was ready to fill in for injured colleagues, to jump into Piper Cubs with his raincoat flapping, thence to soar out over the Finger Lakes, the Adirondacks, Ni-agara, to get at more and more campuses. He couldn't have enough of dappled sandstone buildings, mild-eyed deans in violet gowns, puce tippets, and mystifying insignia; the works.

The Academy, vague woolly womb, he had been away too long. He was at first peeved by the spring riots, which threatened the cardboard sets of the preposterously bogus American college, but now saw that they were in the nature of a festival. The students crouched in doorways, smiling and chatting and exulting in the sunshine. They were keeping people out of the winter buildings, they explained, or trapping the bad ones inside; they waved placards at Max demanding new gyms or denouncing new gyms as the case might be. He waved back or stopped and asked what was eating them. They seemed happy to chat about their grievances with anyone who would listen.

Max listened. He listened to everybody. A mental breakdown, if that was the word, occupied such a small part of your mind. Now he wanted to hear from the rest of the world, to flood himself with other people's concerns. He listened to liberal professors and harassed authorities and intensely reasonable rebels, and sympathized with all of them, on no special principle. They all seemed like very nice people, and he felt that everything was going to be all right.

His lectures were fairly bland, by his standards, and more scholarly than he had been for years. He had missed all that lately. He got excited about Aeschylus and the development of the Greek chorus. Angry young students stood in the back and shouted "Irrelevant" and Max shouted back, "That's what you need, you people, a little irrelevance in your lives. That's what civilization

233

is all about." Talking to other people, what a pleasure, after a winter of gnawing on bones. "Every time you people go to the can, it has to be relevant. You are here to learn about something else—about decoration, about drawing the first picture in your cave and singing a song that is not an attack on the neighboring chieftain." The kids shook their heads. The poor lambs thought that their *gymnasium* was relevant. They would learn.

After one of his talks a man came up and said, "You know, you're not really like your writing at all. You're really a nice guy." And although the man was an undoubted little twit, Max was touchingly pleased. They were nearly all twits, Max had not lost his judgment, but they were good, kind twits.

Back in the city, Max resumed the shakes. He had lost his children. There was no hope in his life. One had to treasure a few good moments. He understood that he was in no shape to take over the children's custody, could barely manage his own. It was best to stay out of their lives entirely, and hope that his genes would do them some good some day.

His final appearance of the season was at Winslow University, where he was entertained by his old classmate, Graham Woodcock, who ran the English department. Woodcock looked about twenty-two, to Max's one hundred, which was depressing. They sat in Woodcock's study, and Max drank and Graham didn't.

"Haven't you had enough yet?" said Graham, who had reviewed around for a couple of years, before ducking out.

"I don't know. How much is enough?" Max, having no equals, had talked to no one about this. He had de-

234

spised Woodcock particularly—slinking off to the Academy like that, before his wounds had even begun to show. But there was something to be said for looking twenty-two.

"It reads to me as if you've had enough," said Graham. "Your pieces sound bored."

"How about your lectures?"

"Yes, well, nobody hears them except a select few. And, I don't know, every year is a new beginning, isn't it? Fresh faces . . ." Oh Christ, the joys of teaching. Did they all have to whimper like this about the Young? Max felt a last movement of rage, like a stirring of old tea leaves.

"There's no such thing as a fresh face," said Max. "Every feature has been done into the ground by now, and you know it."

"You're probably right," said Graham. "I suppose I'm recruiting you to share my misery. Isn't that the point of recruiting?"

"Recruiting me." Max looked around wildly at the academic study with the academic furniture and the endless bloody books. Even so, the bear looks down at his trap.

"Yes, away from all those expense accounts and parties and onto the great sheepskin tit."

He didn't look any twenty-two. "Why aren't you drinking?" said Max sharply.

"I gave it up. It made me nervous."

Just as I thought. Things can get jumpy around the sheepskin tit, too. Woodcock screwed his face into an expression of diplomacy. "It isn't a question of liking it, Max. It's a question of refueling. You are undoubtedly the best-equipped critic of our generation." I won't listen, I won't listen. "But you've never quite fulfilled your promise, have you? Our fault, no doubt, for expecting the moon. But that's what you expected, too, isn't it?"

How would you like a punch in the mouth. No, I've done that. Look, Woodcock, let's get one thing clear. If I come to this fucking sheep dip, it is not to improve myself. It is because I have given up. It is because there is no hope. I'll become smooth and soft like you. Because I can't do what I wanted to. I'm not man enough any more. O.K., is that understood, you smirking little rabbit?

"You can do some real criticism, long pieces, monographs . . ."

No, you don't understand yet, do you? Let me explain again. I fell off my horse, I broke my neck. I am applying for admission to your hospital as a bona fide cripple.

"Do I sense that you're weakening?"

Yes, yes. Now you've got it. "It's very tempting," said Max. He saw himself smiling encouragement to the freshman cliché faces, being a nice guy—it took so little. That used to be Max Jamison over there. Retired man of action. Once he talked about riding the arts like a whirlwind. Now he composes monographs. On little embroidery hoops.

"Your wife will like it here, if she doesn't mind being a teeny bit bored."

Max laughed and laughed. "She doesn't mind that at all," he said finally, then added, "Tell me, Woody, do I get to teach girls?" Woodcock joined uneasily in the mirth.

236

"Old critic lumbering out to stud. Becoming middle-aged is such a convulsion—one heard it was going to be bad, but not this bad. What's wrong with teaching, I'll tell you what's wrong with teaching. Every gray-faced mediocrity you meet turns out, on examination, to be a teacher. Even in the theater— If you see a young character who teaches or wants to teach, or an old character who teaches or has taught, you know you're up against some sort of dreary little fart right away. There are no exceptions to this. Teaching is the American for second-rate. Tenure, department, credits—a tray of gelding devices for the old bull."

Max would not even bother to mail this. There was no need to share every thought with others. Being a magazine writer had unbalanced him in this respect. First serial rights to his thoughts belonged to himself.

"Pros and cons. Hatred of the Academy may be a bit irrational. Feeling they've been judging you all these years. If I can become prof, I can judge *other* Jamisons. Have earned that right. And I can shape the silly-putty features of the young into sneering corroboration. Thus to pass my maturity. But there's another side to this, Mrs. Bloom, sir, that you're forgetting. You envy the Academy, don't you? When a troubled young teacher from Madison, Wisconsin, who writes with a lisp, says that all the New York critics have missed the point about Brecht, you fear he may be onto something. You have lived off your reflexes too long. This cosseted castratus has paid, with his balls, for the time to think."

Max stopped typing. It seemed now like an awful effort to peck out the words if nobody was going to see them. The last phrase actually read "time to thnk" and he had dallied over the "n" in "thnk," wondering whether even that was strictly necessary.

How quietly one set of worries replaced another. The teaching thing had superseded whatever the last thing was, without a sound. And when teaching grew stale, he could give up smoking and moan about that. Or devise an ingenious health problem. The secret of middle age would be to hustle his worries from place to place, searching always for tolerable locations. A slipped disk would be fine for autumn. Then a fear of fascism for Christmas. And so to the grave.

"It wnt angr that I tk to plys," he typed. Anger was a later distortion, dilution if you will, of the critical passion. When he began just getting angry, he should have known he was nearly finished. Grumpy old curmudgeon now, with no harm in him. Which meant, it suddenly occurred to him, that if the day was warm and he wrapped up carefully, he could probably visit Justin. There was nothing stopping him. He was like a grandfather now, and nobody was afraid of grandfathers. It would be nice to see Justin again . . . But hard as he tried, he could picture him as no more than a pleasant small boy, like many others. He wasn't sure he didn't slightly prefer Charlie. Christ, one paid a price for peace.

What is this book here? A heartwarming pile of shit —Mr. Jamison, you're too much; salty and deliciously irreverent; bad language, all that's left of the old volcano. Eight hundred words, due by Monday. It was a terrible book, but there was no point in hurting the author's feelings. Never strike a child except in anger, as

Bernard Shaw said, and he felt no anger. So he wrote a kind review, tasting with a sour face the letter to come: "You are the first person to really understand my work. I heard you were a rat, but you know, you're a real person, Mr. Jamison."

Gene Mungo said, "We don't seem to be doing much for each other now, do we?" If he hadn't chosen that moment to hit his dreary guitar, she might have brought up an argument. As it was, she shrugged and continued to make the bed under him.

"Max held us together as long as he could, but now his letters are boring as hell. And you're just holding the line. I don't exactly turn you on any more, do I?"

"No one can be turned on all the time."

"Yeah. But I like them to try." He hit the guitar again, a tic that drove her to distraction. "You're not concentrating, baby. Either you leave your husband or you don't. I'm tired of finding him in the umbrella stand every morning."

She smiled in spite of herself. "Are you really a primitive, Gene? Or did you, as I suspect, go to Harvard Business School?"

"No one's born primitive, baby. Not in this country, anyway. You have to work at it."

He was sweet. It was unthinkable to get mad at him. Talking to him was sweet and funny and quite pointless. "It'll be a wrench leaving the bed, won't it?" she said.

"That's always the hardest part." He swung his legs over the side. "See, there we go. It can be done." Just like that, he began to collect his stuff. Could this heart-breaking scene actually be painless? For people like Gene, apparently it could. And if for him, why not for her?

"I have to get out before Justin bites me," he said, stuffing dirty clothes into his knapsack. "You're on the road to health, I can tell."

"You don't want to try a little longer?"

"Oh no, baby, not at *all*." He shook his head in a slow wide arc. "The time is *now*. Otherwise, we waste another ten years, right? When love is gone, it's replaced by this cheap glue, very strong."

"How did you ever have time to learn that?"

"I read it in a Christmas cracker. But you weary of my great wisdom. It's time to push off."

He kissed her once, with a smiling mouth, and a minute later he was out in the back yard, shouting for the boys to come and say goodbye.

The country retreat didn't make much sense after that, but neither did going back to the city. She had the place to herself and enough money from Max to run it, and she was happy to concentrate on that, the world of things, and forget people for a while. What do you do next, join a dating service, go on a cruise? If Max was really dead, she could collect his papers and become a Jamison expert. As it was, she volunteered to help out in the local summer-camp program, where she found herself refereeing softball games and holding small children under the stomach while they flapped and wriggled their way to swimming mastery. Her ideal husband now would be a nice rich naturalist twenty years her senior, who had nothing to teach her except the patterns on butterflies. Or perhaps she should take up teaching herself. Pass on the lessons of Max and Gene to a younger man, as they did it in France. Justin perhaps? In a nice non-Oedipal way, of course.

She began to undergo violent spasms of optimism about her life. The forties and fifties could be a prime for American women if they didn't get flustered. So many friends had given up too soon because of stupid husbands and stupid lives, and were out of the running. She, on the other hand, had never ceased learning and growing. She owed Max something for that, poor dear, and Gene something else; and herself something, too, for picking instructive men. Now, what was it to be? Social work? Back to college for the old M.A.? What did those women with the vague aura of competence and success do? (She had not lost her sense of humor about herself.)

While trying to make up her mind, she dashed off an ardent little essay about a child's discovery of nature. She had sighted Charlie staring at a robin's egg and had taken it from there. She sold it to a women's magazine under her maiden name of Helen MacKintosh, and prepared to write another one.

It could almost have been her distinguished older man himself, getting out of the taxi as though his lap was a slight problem. He must have gained a good twenty pounds and there were iron bars in his hair. His walk was slower, more stately. Altogether, impressive. A President's committee on the arts kind of walk.

Max had written to warn of his coming. There was no belch of smoke as she had opened the envelope. He apologized briefly for those letters. A slight brainstorm from overwork, he explained. He was much better now that he had left the magazine. Very much better. Oh, and best to Gene.

"Open the damn door," said the old Max. But the new one just gazed around mildly at the parched, late-summer lawn. The prowl had gone out of his stance; the caged lion looked fed and rested. Still, she couldn't stand here at the upstairs window indefinitely.

"Hello, Helen." She didn't want to look in his eyes at first. The brainstorm had blown them out, she knew it. His mouth would form a thin line like her mother's in the funeral parlor. "How are you?" he asked. They shook hands carefully.

Next they sat down in the living room. The kids were out back, she believed. He had presents in his briefcase for them. Hoped they were suitable.

She said that Gene had left. He nodded diplomatically. It was like talking to the delegate from Kenya. There was nothing wrong with his face. It was fuller and in some ways more youthful. He looked as if he had many good years ahead of him.

"I'm very excited about teaching," he said. (Max? excited? Must be a joke.) "I found that my standing with the academics was much higher than I thought. I actually had a choice of jobs, even though it was already summer. All that worry about nothing." He paused, then rumbled on. "It's a fine department at Winslow. Several first-rate men. And they tell me the students . . ."

She stared in disbelief. A bore! God, no, it couldn't be. Was this what she had asked for? She had requested him to change, to grow, but this was a damnable trick. He smiled slightly; I hope you're satisfied, my dear. "Yes, it'll be nice teaching again. I've always liked Winslow. My old friend Graham Woodcock is there. The workload is reasonable, eight hours a week." Yes, yes—there were years and years ahead of him.

"That's nice, Max. It truly is."

"I feel as if I've been reborn," he said. "I may be old as a critic, but I'm young as a teacher. In fact, I'm really in my prime, you know. You may laugh, but I've decided to get back to my Ph.D. thesis."

That's the last time I ask anyone to change, she thought. And yet there was something sickly attractive about all this. He was going to press on and become an outstanding academic. She saw him doing the celebrity shuffle down some shaded walk, black gown worn casually, satirically. Dean Jamison, author of *The Once and Sometime Theatre*, and *Drama as Liturgy, Liturgy qua drama: Homer to Aeschylus*. It took her back to school, too. All good Americans go back to school eventually. Max had made such a great show of leaving, had kicked off the dust, shaken both fists, roared and bellowed like a swamp animal; and now he was re-enrolling for the fall semester, with his pennant and his beanie.

A dean needs a wife, a dean needs a wife, heigh-ho the dairy-oh—she couldn't help it, but she was already halfway into the picture herself. Wife of Head of the Department. Writing her nature pieces. Spring lays its tawny fingers on Winslow. Max would not be too sexually demanding, she could tell. Psychologically, they were suitably separated now as most middle-aged couples were. And it would be good for the children.

There was nothing *intrinsically* wrong with being practical; even for an old English major.

He smiled again, as if his courtship was going famously. The old prof had worked up some new tactics. "Ortega said that the years between forty-five and sixty are the years of mastery," said Max. "I always thought that that was just Ortega's little joke. But I see what he meant now. What he didn't say was how much blood you lost along the way." Helen would have to think about this. A *likable* Max? How perverse can you get, said the old Max, in her head. But that was the only place he existed any more, in her head. Narcissus had grown old, but his face lingered in the pool.

The first thing Justin thought was, I'm not afraid of that voice. Then as he jogged over the grass toward his father, he remembered for just a second. There was something about the dark outline under the tree branch that would save him and fill his days with sweetness. It was gone with the next jog, the slightest movement is enough to jar such thoughts, but it sent him catapulting at Max with pure longing. The big hands trembled for a moment on his shoulders, and then arms were squeezing the breath out of him. "You weigh a ton," said Max, putting him down at last.

Charlie, who might be assumed not to give a damn, and possibly didn't, came rolling up and said, "You came back," and found a place on Max's trouser leg and hung there, next to his brother in simple contentment, until Max picked him up and carried him on his shoulder inside, with Justin trotting alongside.

part five

25

Winslow University was a good place to recuperate. It proved to have a soft downy atmosphere like traveling second-class on a Cunard ship. Afternoon tea, with a blanket round your knees; semi-classics for your listening pleasure; the complete works of John Buchan in the ship's library; and at night—Bingo! at the captain's table. The decks were lined with dozing critics of Society, dying or just pretending.

The muscles in the amputated pitching arm began to twitch slightly with the start of a new season. When the drama school put on a Brecht cycle, Max lashed it the old way in the Winslow *Quarterly*. A black Macheath stripped to the waist—well, he tried to be tactful about that. But the orgy in *Baal* reminded him of the croquet

finals at Brighton-on-the-Wold, and he said so bluntly:
to young actors with trembling chins, and a bristling,
mouth-working-fitfully dean. "Does Mr. Jamison think
he can do better?" "No, Mr. Jamison has more sense
than that. Mr. Jamison doesn't think he can play quar-
terback either."

In this little culture reserve, that kind of exchange
seemed worth plugging through again. Some students
thrilled to one; others snarled and muttered words like
"glib"; impressionable coeds burst into tears. Fight
fiercely, Jamison; it really matters at Winslow. It was in
such a world of make-believe that he had received his
calling in the first place. One played criticism deadly
seriously on campus. It was like believing in squash. His
mistake had been taking his college spirit down to New
York with him.

An ex-critic can tell from his mailbox how much he
used to be valued. Within two days of retirement, Max's
was windswept and empty: leaving him to understand
that nobody on Broadway or in Hollywood had ever
given a damn what he thought. While he was being so
desperately judicious, they thought he was just showing
off, or settling scores. That was what made his whole career so touching. All that integrity and nobody cared.
Up here, of course, they cared like mad.

All the same, Winslow was soon getting on his nerves.
Perhaps he had picked up a touch of Broadway himself
without noticing; at any rate, the devil put thoughts in
his head like, well, who does give a shit what Graham
Woodcock thinks about the Elizabethan lyric? The
country was all lopsided, too much vulgarity in one end,
and not enough in the other. As he lined up in the god-

forsaken cafeteria, looking at all the mild myopic faces, an optometrist's paradise, he thought, Go to New York, you timid buggers; go at least to New Haven.

He went to New York himself during the winter vacation to give the bacchanalian whoop-de-do of the New Theatre a flutter. The boys in his class were all agog about participation and body rubbing. Certainly, if the Old Theatre was as tired as its critics were, it was the least he could do. Though as he reached for his fly, he wondered whether this was really theater? Not that it might not be fun in its own right.

He hunkered down on the floor next to a passable girl in black leotards, and decided the success of the play depended on whether he could make out with her. A fragile basis for drama. Max had kept his underpants on out of very pride and thought several fellow bacchantes would have been advised to do likewise. Art was issued with the first pair of pants. There is no art in a nudist colony. He reached casually for the leotards, hoping to seem spontaneous and spirited, but the girl must have spotted the old-fashioned lecher behind the mod gesture, because she writhed out of harm's way.

The others were so dowdy that you couldn't possibly blow your mind with them. They reminded him of slum hallways, and the smell of cabbage, of long johns flapping on a line outside, of trains to and from Hoboken. He decided to crawl after the leotards and then give up. "I'm Max Jamison, shall we go to my place?" was the only truly spontaneous, life-enhancing phrase he could think of. But her legs carried her crabwise away. A young man stared up at him ardently, looking for Daddy, no doubt—you've come to the wrong church, my son. Out of my way, please, while I hunt for daughter. But just then a fat girl jumped him playfully and almost cracked his spine.

As he lay there gathering breath, he thought for the first time in several years how much he actually loved the theater. This galumphing horseplay might be all right in a German military school. And all this fuck talk that the fat girl was cooing into his ear. A very good fuck fuck fuck to you, too, madam. And oink and grunt while we're about it. If this bag would just get off him, he could think more clearly. The big girl went romping off at last, leaving him more dead than alive.

"Critics like you are all uptight," he could hear all the little men screaming now. "You're scared of your bodies, scared of life. So you make up excuses. You rediscover tradition, for Godsake."

So that's what you think, eh? Max would show them something. He looked around for the girl in the leotards, but she had gone. Looked down at himself and saw that he was too old to go hunting in jockey shorts. So he just sat there with the other misfits, waiting for the peripeteia.

"The theater of Flesh is a great force for decency," he told his class when he got back. "After a session there, a normal man resolves (1) to clean up his language, and (2) to hang onto his pants at all times. No, I was not embarrassed. At a certain age, embarrassment seems to cease. I can't explain why. Like all youthful encumberments, one misses it at times. Bored? Not especially. Not more than usual. It gives you a chance to think, like being in the army. Yes, it also drives one back to the traditional theater (do you think that's why they're doing it?). So they tell you that rediscovering tradition is a fake, like a deathbed conversion to a boring religion. Still, you *have* rediscovered it, fake or no, and that's the main thing."

He heard, or thought he heard, the usual whispers. "Glib." "Sell-out." "Fantastic." They were probably saying the same things about Aristotle.

One last chance, Youth. He checked their faces out carefully. So many of his contemporaries gushed about the Kids these days—brighter than we were, more mature (although why go to kids if you were looking for that?), more eager, etc., etc. To an aging critic, a year's teaching was good for at least one rebirth; like visiting a whorehouse. Wrong image. Like marrying a child bride. In either event, there was something unhealthy about such health. Sucking life from the children. Worse, from other people's children. Probably better to admit you're dead. Still, he preferred them to the other professors.

As spring came round, he considered assembling the college on some ruse and staging a sex-cum-ideas riot— at the end of which he could sprint through the gates bare-assed, brandishing a torch. But Max was deeply committed to his pants by now, and decided he must operate from that bastion. A thought for the class: "Jokes lose in execution. Action belongs in the mind." He said it mainly to shock them, but found that the idea pleased him. "I can imagine a dozen spring revels in the time it takes you to stage one." And the fate he imaged for the college president was of an aesthetic delicacy that no cast of sheltered college actors could hope to achieve.

"How about the unpredictable?" said Master Bones in the audience. "How about the existential? That's what makes action superior to thought."

Max cuffed him playfully. "My imagination is quite unpredictable enough. More so than your body, I venture to guess."

"Yes, but. Yes, but. We aren't just bodies, are we? Our action is our thought. In a sense, I mean. A lot of people doing their things at once produces, I don't know . . ."

Max rocked back in half sleep. What a great substitute this was for being alive. "Utter predictability," he chimed in. "Science assures us that collections of atoms are more accountable than individual ones."

The pink-faced nucleus before him strove to say something unaccountable.

"What about the breath of life, Dr. Jamison? What about sweat and the touch of other bodies?"

I thought you'd say that. Actually, I left the touch of bodies some time ago. It didn't work too well. "I don't know. Try it. But you didn't come to me to learn about that, did you?" he said.

Was there a young Max Jamison in his class? Did he want one? Young critics should probably be drowned with their first quizzical squeal. There was a saturnine fellow called Parfitt who seemed to be copying Max's style, but that eliminated him immediately. Real Jamisons imitate nobody. A midgety little chap called Harris seemed closer, a Jamison for the seventies, believing the opposite of Max on every single point. But he was too short.

Max asked Harris if he wanted to be a critic when he grew up, and he said, "Christ, no." Was that what a Jamison for the seventies would say?

Max had to see a certain amount of Graham Woodcock, because they were supposed to be friends. Woodcock could still be taunted into believing in what he was doing; and so Max bounced him around idly.

"Woodcock, they won't spare you when their revolution comes, if that's what you're thinking. They might possibly keep me in a cage, like Gargantua. But fellow-travelers like you will have no use at all."

He wasn't really saying this for the sake of Graham, who bored him down to the fine hair on his toes, but for Julia Woodcock, a former student of Graham's and now his wife. He did not especially wish to bed her, not with those knees, but he did want to impress her. The desire to please women was no doubt at the beginning of all art and thought. (What a silly misunderstanding, if so.) He also wanted to impress Elsie Merriman while he was about it, and Wilma Pfaff, other professors' wives of passable appearance. Naturally, the more he impressed the girls, the more he annoyed their husbands. But that was the rhythm of life. It would be fun to fight a duel with a maddened professor some day, properly gowned, in front of the whole school. And then scamper off to the bell tower, cackling.

At the end of the spring semester, his enemy Harris came slumping up, to deliver the goofiest sentence of the year, "You're all right, Mr. Jamison. You understand kids."

Max hit the desk with his palm. "That's nice of you, Harris. I always felt that the most overrated quality of your generation was its insight. Now I know it. You're stone blind, Harris. 'You can't fool the kids,' they say. Good God, they're easier to fool than psychiatrists."

"Maybe." Harris was indomitably good-natured. "But we dig you anyway. You're the kind of man some of us wouldn't mind being."

Max basked briefly and hoped that this made some kind of sense; that he had by zany coincidence arrived at the same place they had. No American, however pedophobic—not the great W. C. Fields himself—could be really sorry to hear that the kids were on his side.

But he couldn't fool himself. He didn't believe in miracles. Harris was looking at him with blind animal friendliness, that was all. Max could not return it. He knew too much.

"If you think that, you haven't understood a word I've said. Ideas mean nothing to you."

"Yeah. Maybe that's it." Harris abruptly walked away.

"Good luck," said Max, but Harris didn't look round.

After giving the lowest marks he was allowed to give to all the class but three (Harris wrote him a note: "Man, was I wrong about you. You must be a really unhappy person"), he signed up with *Rearview* to resume his theater chores there. It wasn't fair to go on taking up a hospital bed at Winslow. His old replacement had moved over to *Worldfacts:* a sell-out, poor devil. (Hope his wife understands.) Now if Bruffin would just catch on with a big foundation, happiness would be complete. Jack Flashman, who had expected the *Worldfacts* job, had gone, muttering, over to *Backchat* instead, the show-business bible. So Max clambered into the empty chair.

Epilogue

Max commutes to Broadway as often as five times a week in the busy season, feeling a bit like his father going to work at the bank. Sometimes he even treats himself to a rented car. He can afford to do this because Helen's book, *Garden Adventure*, had earned a good advance and been selected by one of the book clubs. Having left the drugged air of Winslow, they bought a house in Fairfield County. Justin has turned into an average thug and they never see him any more: the book says this is correct for his age. Charlie now seems the more sensitive of the two. Max fusses over them both guardedly and even writes down their sayings. He does not want to make them uncomfortable with his attention.

As to his work, he tells stray acolytes that anyone who takes criticism seriously these days is a blundering idiot. His first book, *The Fallacy of the Post-Modern,* bores him already and may never be finished. He writes careless pieces now, and even puts in mistakes to see if anyone notices. Nobody does. "I was much more serious at *Now.* A sell-out has responsibilities," he tells his latest phantom interviewer—an aging but sprightly librarian. (If he gooses her occasionally, it is out of kindness.) His mail tells him he is spiteful, heartless, and kind of wonderful, about as before. At an average eleven letters a year, it doesn't make too much difference. "I won't play the sap for anyone, Miss Frisby," he says, teasing shamelessly. Librarians believe you should do your best even if no one in the world is watching.

His departure from *Now* has automatically doubled his status with the few who care. Although he has not done a really good piece in over two years now, he finds himself referred to more and more often as "our leading drama critic." Simply hanging around seems to do this —a discovery that might have saved some pain earlier. He has been asked to serve on the Presidential Committee on the Arts, to judge young playwrights on the West Coast and old ones for the Pulitzer people, and could probably committee around the clock if he felt like it. He assumes that this pleases Helen, that it looks to her like movement and progress. So he keeps adding little clusters of junk to his recent listing in *Who's Who,* for the sake of peace. He doesn't want her taking the children away again.

Little fear of that. She didn't like his leaving Winslow at first. But a dean of critics is better than no dean at all, and she seems to find the new Max tolerable. He never criticizes anything in front of her now, and she confides that she finds him much more civilized than before. Success has mellowed her, and Max gets no trouble from her end of the house. "She doesn't talk about life any more—she talks about maturity," he has been heard to observe. He is a son of a bitch in an imperfect world.

" 'Why?' is a question that no man in his right mind asks himself, unless he has the answer rigged," says Jamison, and he means it. But when the librarian persists, he points to the odd times when he takes Charlie to a movie, or just bumbles into his bedroom for a talk, and the memory comes back of going to meet the Arts, hand in hand, with his father. Like other people's Sunday churchgoing: a little too grave to be fun. Yet with flashes of wild, dirty joy, as you touched the sacrament. To see this joy now in the faces of his sons would be pretty good—perhaps a little better than anything he still expects to get from women. He will do nothing to risk losing this. Christ, he will even praise his wife's books, if necessary. Will you buy that, librarian?

Jack Flashman came over recently (they're friends now, about like old army buddies), and Charlie said to one of Jack's sleazy-looking boys, "My father is wiser than your father." Never mind what he thinks the word means, Max liked the line. The kind of thing he used to wring out of babes he now gets for free.

"How come you and Helen got together again?" Flashman asked. He is the only friend crass enough to ask this kind of question, which is what makes him so necessary.

"I'll give you two theories about that," said Max,

"both equally superficial. One is that she doesn't mind me a bit, now that she can support me. I'm a distinguished appendage, and how many women have one of those? Nasty? you bet. But that's my critical style, and my life must conform to it. Another theory, Helen's, is that I need her. That I cracked up when I lived by myself and would do so again. I need approval on a steady basis, as I get older. Like a weekly pay check."

Flashman nodded. "Superficial, huh?"

"Oh, sure. It's the kind of thing people say about each other all the time. It's the best they can do in the way of analysis. Critics do it better. Would you like a couple of other theories?"

"God, no. Let me know if you come to something you really believe. What about the boys?"

One confessed to Flashman finally, because out of the jumble, he had emerged as the Spirit of Broadway, and one owed him an explanation. "Charlie came out of the year better. Justin got hurt by it. I mean my feeling about Justin got hurt. You don't understand that, I trust. How about you and the ladies, by the way?"

Jack formed a ring with his finger and thumb and nodded solemnly.

Flashman also took part in a recent chess-puzzle fantasy. There isn't a piece exactly right for Jack, chess being a dignified game. So Max made him the black knight, with the circumscribed field and the little dogleg pounce. Old Professor Godfrey was the white bishop, lumbering great distances obliquely.

BISHOP: I don't know what to say. My assistant Plinth says he's gone over to you people. A Broadway intellectual.

KNIGHT: Hah. Try telling that to Broadway.

BISHOP: What do they say over there? Don't they want him either?

KNIGHT: They say that for an egghead, he's a pretty good showman, and for a showman, he's—

BISHOP: Stop. For the last time, I won't have you insulting my Max. He may have made mistakes, of course. But deep down he's a highbrow, I tell you.

KNIGHT (*dancing away*): He's a clown, a fool . . . Got his ideas from the class of '42, a terrible year for ideas, and tries to foist them on the seventies. (*Misses a clumsy swipe from* BISHOP's *crozier.*) He's too precious for Broadway, too stiff for Off-Broadway. He's like some old professor on the Bowery. Hasn't cracked a book in thirty years. But still—he's the *Professor!* Christ, he's worse than *you!*

The Bishop advances unsteadily, on his vulnerable path. The black knight jumps crookedly onto his pale back. They scuffle briefly. Max does the next part himself, so it's all in fun. The bishop lies on the carpet, in real life this time, with his wooden head twisted off.

afterword

"Who is Max Jamison?" This peculiar question has followed me ever since I wrote a novel of that name about a critic who couldn't turn off his engine, but kept on reviewing everything in sight from his furniture to his family to, most brilliantly and brutally, himself. Max was nothing if not fair.

Since readers seem to prefer true stories to made-up ones, and since I was getting kind of curious myself, I tried for a while actually answering the question, in hopes of surprising myself with the truth. But none of the names I came up with, from Alexander Woollcott

Written as the Introduction to the COMMON READER EDITION of *The Morning After . . . and Long After*, published simultaneously with *Max Jamison*.

to Pauline Kael to Flaubert's ever-popular "Jamison, *c'est moi*" quite seemed to fit, including, thank God, my own, as was proved once and for all, I trust, by my first collection of reviews and stuff called *The Morning After*, which came out not long after Max, and which the Akadine Press is now obligingly reissuing alongside it. Max most decidedly did not write "stuff" and would not have approved a single word of mine, even if I'd stayed with my working title of *Kiss the Blood Off My Typewriter*, which he had perhaps inspired himself.

"So Max Jamison is a composite, right?" For a piece that may possibly run, space allowing, on the last page of next month's Arts roundup, this discussion has probably gone on quite long enough, and the above sentence seems to be universal interview-speak for "time's up!" Now if you'll just agree to this obvious proposition . . .

But to an unknown writer (as which writer is not these days?), one more line in the *Podunk Picayune* is always worth shooting for. So one day, I finally decided to answer this question too. "No, he's not a composite," I said, "he's an essence."

Eureka! "Max Jamison is a composite," the man wrote anyway, but I *had* surprised myself after all with the whole secret of writing novels, my novels anyhow. You just hang around a subject, professional, political, domestic, for a few years or minutes until you suddenly get the gist of it and then without consciously thinking about it again, you turn on the dream machine and start taking notes. And pretty soon a voice will come in. Who *is* this and what does he want? Never mind. Keep him

talking and maybe he'll give himself away, plus possibly
the person he's talking to, and, if you're really hot today,
maybe some décor and an indefinable smell. And by
the time you're done, someone will tell you that you
have just written a perfect description of a person
you've never met and a place you've never been.

Thus, after the inevitable treading of water and
crossing of burning sand for the usual 100 years or so,
one arrives at a complete Max Jamison; and once he's
on the page, he's also on his own. Your guess about him
by now is at least as good as mine—and maybe as good
as his too. Because although Max much prefers to talk
for himself and have the last word, I'm not sure he ever
gets himself quite right. People seldom do.

My own reviewing life is quite another story. In fact,
I myself might very well be a composite. My first reviewing self was simply a common-or-garden kibitzer
trolling for laughs. A friend named Ed Rice had asked
me to cover movies for his highbrow Catholic picture
magazine, if you can imagine such a thing, called *Jubilee*, and I told him I hadn't seen a movie in three
years. "That's great," he said. "Just make some jokes."
And, he added reassuringly, "They don't even have to
be about movies."

That was simply what you did with movies in the late
1950s. *Jubilee* could be deadly serious about the other
arts, as I learned when I tried cracking some jokes
about Giacometti as well. But when it came to Hollywood, you were expected to smirk and roll your eyes
to heaven; it was a proof of your own seriousness—
until, that is, the mid-1960s, when the movies them-

selves suddenly became a very serious subject, and my jokes, which by then I was making for *Esquire*, seemed as dated as an old grad with a funny hat and a noise-maker. ("You have the finest mind in the 18th century," snarled one reader. "You're too kind," I answered. "I'm not that good.")

But meanwhile, I had found a much more congenial form of criticism, to wit theater reviewing, which is far and away the most exacting and exciting kind of criticism there is. You can doze off at a film, and fall dead asleep over a book, and no one need ever know; but one lapse of attention at a play can snap the thread and cost you the whole evening. A play is a single experience that has to be taken at a single sitting. And if you miss a line, it's no use asking someone else to tell you about it. The whole carpet has unraveled and you just have to go back and start over again.

Each time you see a play is a distinct experience too. The cast is in a different phase and so are you. A play doesn't just sit there like a book, but comes to unpredictable life again and again. And, as at sports events, you, the spectator, feel like part of what's happening. Actors know within moments what kind of audience they're working with tonight, even before it has uttered a sound, while the first misplaced cough probably sounds like a tray of glasses crashing.

So there you sit, straining every capillary not to cough, sneeze, or daydream—above all, not to snore— all of which can seem sinfully tempting in the green-house air of Broadway theater. And, you're expected to *write* about this? Never mind. Just often enough a great production will come along and turn the whole nerve-wracking procedure to a pure excitement that you can ride home on like surf, as if your review too were now part of the event.

After that, movie reviewing seems like a vacation in, well, would you believe Perth Amboy, New Jersey? While doing it perfectly is probably out of the question because there is too much to talk about, doing it adequately is a snap for the same reason. Nobody seems to care which ball of wool you chase. Critics who decide to devote their entire space to the art of Bugs Bunny or Hitchcock's use of the close-up are probably doing their job as well as anyone else, for at least two good reasons. (1) Movies are modernist despite themselves and no matter how conventional they try to be, plot summaries and cast roundups will always seem to miss the point. The key *has* to be somewhere else, and maybe Hitchcock's close-ups are exactly the place to look. And (2) people go to the movies to see Tom Hanks and Julia Roberts, period. They read you to rap, or be rapped at, about movies. There is little or no connection.

Not so with books. For several years I had been reviewing these too, without considering this a serious occupation. Reviewing each other is the jury duty of the literary life: we simply pass the pencil round and round, drawing a wobbly line each time between the appearance of log-rolling and the real possibilities of envy or contempt. But things get tenser as you approach the top, and as my own assignments became more important, I suddenly found myself making friends and enemies for life with people who might, among other things, someday be reviewing *me*, with either transparent flattery or heart-felt hatred, a bad bet either way. Although one author, whose book I liked, jocularly offered me a free heart transplant, something every critic could use, the death threats sounded much more believable.

It was never like this at the movies. In fact, it is probably impossible to hurt a movie's feelings—where do you begin? With the assistant sound coordinator? And it's not all that easy with a play either, unless you write for the next day's newspaper. By the time most magazine reviews appear, the play has either closed, or is so drunk with success that it can't hear you anymore.

But book authors are always tender, even when they're out of print, and success only makes them more so. And no review turns out to be too insignificant to get under their skins and stay there forever. *The Morning After* actually kicks off with a lighthearted piece on this subject, and it certainly does have its comic side. But making enemies is seldom totally funny and as one gets to know one's targets as real people—something academic critics seldom do, which is why they're such killers—one may be subject to regrets and reconsiderations, and here are a couple of mine.

To begin with the easiest, Gore Vidal wrote one of his trademark sniffy notes to the *Times* after my piece came out, but I assumed this was just *pro forma*, like Norman Mailer's genial offer to push me down stairs after some forgotten review of some forgotten book. Vidal's whole style seems to invite and defy attack. Like Muhammad Ali sticking out his chin and pointing to it, Vidal knows he's too fast to get hit, and on a platform I expect he's right. But in print, even the slowest moving battleships must land one occasionally. And whether I did so or not (I'd be the last to know), Gore had no business getting sore about it. He *started* it, by throwing out the first smirk.

My only regret about the piece is my callow view of homosexuality at the time. Of course (a phrase I should perhaps use more carefully) homosexuality is genetic, not chosen; and no, it doesn't always show. Since the great Closet Exodus a few years back, the most amazing people have turned out to be gay, and to use the simile in my original piece—Brooklyn Dodger fans were usually *much* easier to spot.

My other Vidal-related fibrillation, not big enough to call a regret, is that he hadn't yet written, so I hadn't yet read, the best of his historical American novels, *Burr*, *Lincoln*, and *1876*. If I had, I might not only have been a touch more respectful, but might also have recused myself from reviewing William Styron's *Nat Turner*, and spared everyone some grief. When I finally read Henry James's opinion that all historical fiction is more or less humbug, I understood both my Nat Turner problem and my Vidal non-problem perfectly. No one can ever quite recapture the feel and sound of another period. A young writer setting a story as recently as World War II will still get it slightly wrong. So what chance does one have when there's no living memory left to check with? Charles Dickens's version of the cockney dialect in *Pickwick Papers* is totally at odds with Bernard Shaw's in *Pygmalion*, which again is quite unlike anything going around London today. So how can one put words into mouths that made such different sounds? Or even know what the same words meant to them? Garry Wills has shown that practically every phrase in the Declaration of Independence had a slightly different value then than now. So—a whole book?

The Vidal solution, and incidentally that of Robert Graves and a few other English fictorians, is simply to get it as right as one can by steeping oneself in whatever is timeless about one's subjects—Vidal *knows* Washington, Graves knew the Mediterranean—but then, to use the unknowable part as a private playground for one's wit, imagination, and craft to romp around in. Vidal's presidents and congressmen are like Madame Tussaud's waxworks, who come to life every hundred years or so in the *real* twilight zone which *is* history, while *I, Claudius* could pass for an ingenious after-dinner charade devised by scholars. "Okay, you be Livia and I'll be Tiberius and let's see what happens." Sometimes, by a process similar to simultaneous equations in math, some truths may actually be arrived at; but if not, you'll have had and conveyed some fun, and maybe taught somebody something.

However, *Nat Turner* is much too serious to be a game, or have a playground attached to it. The author bets his whole bankroll on getting everything right the first time. And if you can do this with *any* time-place, the old South might very well be it. If, as Faulkner says, "the past isn't even the past" down there, why *shouldn't* Styron have heard what he needed as it hung there in the still air?

And if, to cut to the point, he indeed had, who the hell was I, a New Yorker from London and Sydney, to say he hadn't? Or so at least the author's friends, of which he has an enviable number, argued every time I ran into one for the next few years, until I didn't know what to think, except that the front page of *The New York Times Book Review* is, or was, a sensitive place to try out one's theories of historical fiction, and that the author's own reported rage at my review (which he denied when we met) might have been more than justified by the venue: I'd have been pretty burned up too, although as it turned out, I had done Styron a super-small favor by giving him a white enemy to snarl at to balance all the black ones he may have felt he had to be more polite to.

The matter of venue probably also made some difference to my, I like to believe, genuine post-review friendship with James Jones. The gremlins who attend to these things had contrived for Jim and his jolly wife Gloria to move into my neighborhood not long after *The Morning After* came out, so I decided to get this thing over with right away by confronting the man and taking my medicine. But all he said was, "Well, I was sore as hell at first—but at least you took me seriously as a wrahter [that's how he said it]. And besides, I thought *your* last novel lost its nerve someplace in there."

Well, okay. After mumbling something about maybe my nerves weren't as strong as his, I returned happily to my fence-mending, pointing out that at least I'd given him credit for two good books, to which he quickly added "I think that should be three" and if by this he meant the one he was currently working on, he might well have proved right, if only he'd lived long enough to finish it. As it is, the posthumous remains of his putative third good book, published under the name of *Whistle*, constitute one of those tantalizing fragments like Fitzgerald's *The Last Tycoon* that might or might not have hit the moon.

Anyhow, the bottom line, friendship-wise, may be that I'd reviewed Jim's book in *The Atlantic Monthly*, not the *Times*, and he'd probably been in Paris when it had come out, so who cared?

But appearing in *The Atlantic* did not spare me from my last and most curious specimen. Not so long ago, at a book party for William F. Buckley, Jr., I was accosted by a man I didn't recognize anymore who said, or rather sneered, "I guess there's a statute of limitations, you son-of-a-bitch" and turned on his heel. "Who *was* that?" I asked someone. "Don't you *know*?" someone piped back.

Welcome to the world of Norman Podhoretz, where there obviously *is* no statute of limitations, even after thirty years, and where enemies are forever. In fact, Podhoretz had written a book around then called *Ex-Friends* in which ancient feuds still sound as fresh as this morning's razor cuts. In his own defense, he says this is what happens automatically to anyone who moves politically from left to right. But surely friends so easy to lose are just as easy to forget, and besides can always be replaced by equally superficial ones from the new neighborhood. So why does Podhoretz keep glancing over his shoulder? Nobody is looking back at him anymore. Several of his ex-friends are actually dead by now, and presumably past caring, while the most voluble of the survivors, Norman Mailer, has since diversified in such sedulously up-to-date directions as moon landings, Marilyn Monroe, and Madonna, leaving the old New York cultural wars, if not in the dust bin, at least in the filing cabinet, of history. So what makes Podhoretz think that anyone under 70, or living outside New York, still cares?

And the answer, which seems clear from this sad later book, is that the late '60s must truly have been a traumatic time for him, and that losing all those friends probably hurt like hell, politics or no politics. In which case, I wish I'd kept out of it. Reviewing is not that important. At least mine isn't. Max Jamison may have other views.

Indeed, I began to have qualms about my piece almost before it appeared. *The Atlantic* had a long lead time back then and all I knew about *Making It* so far was that two hyper-ambitious friends of mine told me it might be an important book—and if it *was* important, it was a menace.

Soon after that, though, the assault began, and no human should have to put up with the amount of bile that poured like lava onto Podhoretz's head over the next few weeks. Book reviewing should enact some equivalent to the technical knockout in boxing and simply call such massacres off. And the pain must have been all the worse because to a bizarre extent, Norman *was* his book, so that all the criticism was perforce personal. He had laid himself on the line and lost.

In the weeks after my review appeared, I received a charming letter from Philip Rahv, the king of the New York intellectuals, inviting me to write some more essays just like it for *his* magazine, *Modern Occasions*, and this combined with other small signs of approval

273

from the unofficial New York Family of Ideas and Letters enforced the impression that Podhoretz had made a massive miscalculation and laid an egg with the very people he most admired and had most wanted to impress.

But if so, his comeback would show breathtaking brio and heart-stopping chutzpah. Who *were* these people anyway, except a bunch of knee-jerk liberals? The next year or two would witness a total revision of Podhoretz's cosmology, complete with brand new allies and a spanking new philosophy that one can only call paleo-neo-conservatism, into which he flung himself with zestful rage. He had not really lost friends at all, but had made political enemies, a much more dignified thing to do. As I recall, one also heard the perhaps inevitable rumors of a nervous breakdown around then, but Norman assures us that he had never felt saner than he did at that moment. And while a cynic might be tempted to say "that's great—and how is *Mrs.* Napoleon?," there's a ruefulness about this book that suggests a possible layer of self-awareness and of conscious decision-making that may have been underneath the rubble all along. And a more recent debate between him and Victor Navasky of *The Nation* in *The New York Times* shows him all the way out of his bomb shelter and talking to his enemies again the way a good intellectual should.

Nevertheless, after mulling over Max and pondering Podhoretz, I decided there must be a less morbid and, dare one say, less constipated way of "doing" both Arts and Letters. And in no time, I found myself riffling through the names of old friends whom it would be a pleasure to write about in this vague connection: Stanley Kauffmann, for instance, the gentleman film critic who only turns nasty in print; and the noisy Dwight MacDonald, who bellowed like a bull when he thought you were wrong, but could turn on a dime and start agreeing with you vigorously if you made your point. "And don't let anyone talk you out of it," he might add; and the two almost diametrically opposite drama critics John Simon and Robert Brustein, who, if you could somehow pool their strengths, might make the ideal critic, and who in their quite different ways can both manage to get a positive charge out of negative feedback. Brustein once suggested that Lillian Hellman was actually kept alive by feuds. But one doesn't need to gorge on the things like Hellman to find that an occasional fight can tone up the system wonderfully while keeping one's aesthetic ideas on a war footing where they belong.

But then I remembered a piece I had already published about someone quite different again who made a perfect stage villain, and who has enjoyed both the steamiest of confrontations and the pleasantest of lives by simply scrubbing off his war paint between numbers and wiping away the savage leer and literally sailing away on a literal boat: in short, the complete anti-Jamison and anti-Podhoretz.

No one has ever accused Bill Buckley of taking his ideas any less seriously than Podhoretz takes his, or of not hitting just as hard in argument. Yet he wears his many enemies lightly—*they* may stop talking, but he doesn't—and has even been known to make friends with some of them. Anyway, ideology is no barrier. As the great (what? liberal is too tame a word, radical too programmatic) journalist Murray Kempton lay dying, Buckley, his long-time friend and sparring partner, visited him every day, bearing, among other things, facetious messages from Kempton's friends, including me, who was also hospitalized just then, but mercifully not dying, and receiving things like life-quickening Godiva chocolates from this same Buckley.

So my liking for the man does not mean that I've gone over to his side; it means that I don't have to. You don't need to pass an entrance exam to become Buckley's friend, but if you did, I suspect that the highest marks might go to those of us who disagree with him the most. What fun are people you can't fight with?

Clare Boothe Luce once said that the worst thing about growing old was that she didn't have any "warm, personal enemies" left. I have at least one, and Buckley has dozens, and I'm including him here just for that, as an end piece for both Max and Podhoretz and in memory of Kempton too who was the patron saint of every young journalist who wants to know just how much he can get away with in terms both of prose and sheer orneriness.

If Buckley makes one kind of ending, the next piece "There Goes the Judge" makes a second one that could actually double as a beginning. The very title *The Morning After* had presupposed a world in which reviewers always have precious time to think, and preferably to dream, before talking. As Rilke says, one must open oneself completely to art, which means for critics staying open very late indeed some nights, absorbing the after-tastes and shocks, or the absence of them, and keeping one's opinions at bay until the experience has sunk in as deep as it's going to. *Then* you can talk.

This world seemed to end abruptly for me one day in September of 1988 when the lunch dishes at the Book-of-the-Month Club where I'd been judging books for 15 years, were dramatically cleared away and we were told in effect that we'd been taking too long. The war against Time to Think was underway not just at the Club but all over town. The chain stores suddenly seemed to be sending their new books back the day before they got them, and the publishers were firing them off equally fast to the second-hand bookstores and oblivion, which meant that the only successes now were the instant successes. And just like that, browsing was out, along with talking to the store owner about his favorite poet, and just plain wallowing in the funky miasma of dust and pipe smoke that told you what kind of store you were in, and that time had stopped.

So now it's up to the public to sit down on the tracks and let progress spin its wheels for a while, and there are signs it is doing so by such simple moves as supporting the classic bookstores that do remain so enthusiastically that an author can feel like a rock star in some of them and cruising for old books online and apparently even by leaning on the Book-of-the-Month Club a little. At any rate, the Club has recently responded by announcing the restoration of the judge system, though without the power and without the lunch. Which, of course, misses the point completely, because Time to Think preeminently implies time to eat lunch, and take meaningless strolls and long thoughtful naps as well.

Once these essential preparations are done with, get ready to rumble! Like the sovereign sport of cricket, the old Book Club lunches only looked genteel from a distance—just a group of old-timers sipping sherry by the hour, what harm could they do? Up close, it could actually get so politely intense that occasional executives who dropped by looked as if they'd strayed into midtown traffic at rush hour. The speed of thought practically knocked them over, as would the alleged sherry if they'd tried some (to settle this libel once and for all, I never saw a single drop of sherry the whole time I was at the Club, although they may have used it in cooking).

It wasn't just the lunch that did it, though, but the power to decide things. The late J. Anthony Lukas, who was in on the second and final kill, used to tell me how flat it felt every month to crank up all that machinery just to deliver an opinion. It was like asking a pitcher to go into his full wind-up to throw a cornflake. We needed real stakes out there, real money, for the table to move and the spirits to start talking. And although I never touch the stuff myself, I actually believe that the next big adventure of this sort will occur on the Internet, which already shows all the symptoms of a great bookstore, including lower back pain, mild astigmatism and a compulsion to share your discoveries with strangers. And you can drink, smoke and eat to your heart's content throughout, and even enjoy that most basic of pleasures, the one that makes the whole thing work, reading the same sentence over and over and rolling it on your tongue like wine and absorbing it into your soul. "Shall I compare thee to a summer's day?" "She walks in beauty, like the night." A whole world awaits.

So is Max Jamison online by now? It's a pleasure to say that I haven't the faintest idea.

W. S.
May 2001

COMMON READER EDITIONS

As booksellers since 1986, we have been stocking the pages of our monthly catalogue, A COMMON READER, with "Books for Readers with Imagination." Now as publishers, the same motto guides our work. Simply put, the titles we issue as COMMON READER EDITIONS are volumes of uncommon merit which we have enjoyed, and which we think other imaginative readers will enjoy as well. While our selections are as personal as the act of reading itself, what's common to our enterprise is the sense of shared experience a good book brings to solitary readers. We invite you to sample the wide range of COMMON READER EDITIONS, and welcome your comments.

www.commonreader.com